Noah grabbed a rock with one hand, holding the flashlight with the other. He felt his arm strain as he lowered himself into the water. He took a deep breath right before his head went under the surface. He barely fit into the crack. Noah knew he could hold his breath for more than a minute, but that still was precious little time. He shone the light around. Nothing but rock.

Noah pushed down into the crevice, but it quickly tapered off. He would have to go into the cave itself. Fighting to calm himself, Noah edged out of the crevice. The shark darted nearby. Noah plastered himself against the wall of the cave and froze.

Noah Winter Adventures

The Emerald Quest

Visit
www.reneepawlish.com
for information on Renée's other books.

The Emerald Quest

Renée Pawlish

For Beth Hecker:

This home run is for you.

ACKNOWLEDGEMENTS

The author gratefully acknowledges all those who helped in the writing of this book, especially: Beth Hecker and Beth Treat, editors extraordinaire; Dave Martinache of Colorado Scuba Center, for his diving expertise and insights into diving shipwrecks (any mistakes in the book are mine, not his); Thom Adorney for his suggestions and help in getting this in the hands of readers; a wonderful group of beta readers: Julie Buda, Julie Friend, Thomas Lynch, Sean McMullen, Amy Mumma, Brandon Mumma, Sharon Pollock, Karen Rought, Sharon Stogner, and Emma Velie. If I've forgotten anyone, please accept my apologies.

The Emerald Quest

CONTENTS

CHAPTER ONE

"WE FOUND IT!"

Noah Winter saw the twisted piece of metal jutting from the side of the Spanish steamship a second too late. One moment he was swimming effortlessly beside the *San Isabel*. A moment later, the claw-like piece hooked the oxygen hose of his scuba diving gear.

Fstt!

Noah was jerked to a standstill and his regulator popped out of his mouth. Bubbles rushed out the end of the mouthpiece, racing to the ocean's surface. Suddenly without air, Noah had to act quickly. His dive training kicked in. He held his breath and calmly reached down to his right and grabbed the alternate air source. He cleared the apparatus by exhaling into it, forcing the water out of it. He then started breathing the air again.

Noah smiled. Accident averted. Then he looked up and saw his mother poke her head out of the side of the shipwreck. She had seen him using the alternate air source so she kicked hard with her feet and shot through the water toward him. As she drew close, Noah could see through her facemask. Her eyes were wide with alarm.

Funny, he thought. *She seems really worried about me today.*

Noah gave her an okay signal and nodded his head. Even though he was only thirteen, he had been diving for three years, so he knew what to do in an emergency. Noah puzzled over his mom's reaction. She usually trusted him to take care of himself. Seeing that he was okay, she patted him on the shoulder and gestured that she was going back inside the wreck.

It was a beautiful Tuesday afternoon in August. Noah and his parents, Frank and Riley Winter, were diving the *San Isabel.* The *San Isabel* was a passenger liner built in 1907. She was almost 400 feet long, with a 48-foot beam. When the *San Isabel* ferried the seas, she was solid and sleek, with a steel hull, towering masts, and room for over a thousand passengers. In 1922, during a fierce storm off the small island of Key West, Florida, the ship went down with 312 passengers, 88 crew members, and a cargo of olives and wine.

Noah swam after his mom. She slowed as she came to a doorway on the bridge. Then she gingerly glided through the opening, being careful that her scuba gear did not catch on the doorframe, and she disappeared from view. Noah edged closer, but halted before going inside the wreckage of the ship. Since he was not yet sixteen, he was not allowed to penetrate, or go into, a wreck.

Noah spied his mom as she moved into the bridge, past what was left of the ship's wheel. Her underwater dive light illuminated her way, the beam bouncing off the inside walls like rays of sunlight. Noah glanced around what was left of the *San Isabel*. Over time, the hull had rusted. All the wood had deteriorated and crumbled. The ship was only a shell of what it used to be.

Noah noticed something on the floor inside the doorway. He swam close to the door, peering through his mask at a white object. His curiosity getting the best of him, he moved into the doorway and grabbed the object. As he did, his tank bumped the ship. Noah backed out, his heart racing.

I'd be in big trouble if Mom or Dad saw me do that, he thought.

He examined the piece he'd retrieved. It was a circular piece of white porcelain, like the rim of a cup. It had round edges and there was writing on it. Noah looked more closely. Thin wires stretched across the opening, hooked to tiny screws in each side of the porcelain. It reminded him of a flour sifter, but with most of the wire mesh removed. Noah ran his hand over the piece and wondered about the people on the ship. Did a cook use this? Who were the passengers? Noah pictured a woman, dressed in a pretty full-length dress, dining as she sat across from her husband. She would be dreaming about when the long journey over the ocean would be over. Noah gazed at the wreckage. *Only she didn't make it,* he thought sadly.

Noah looked back inside the wreck. Both his mom and dad had vanished into the innards of the ship. Noah imagined them, with their flashlights illuminating the darkness, poking around the depths of the *San Isabel*. They were searching for a treasure map, although Noah couldn't see how a map of any kind would have survived in the water.

Noah meandered away from the bridge toward the bow of the ship. Above him, through the clear, warm water, he could see the underside of the *Explorer*, the cabin cruiser his parents owned. Sunlight pierced down from the ocean's surface. Noah was in his own little world, where all he heard was the sound of his breathing through the regulator. He had spent countless hours diving with his parents, and he loved being beneath the ocean's surface.

As he wandered about the wreckage, Noah came to a jagged hole in the ship's hull. This damage was what had sunk the ship. The water here was only twenty-five feet deep and the *San Isabel* had apparently run into a reef, sending the crew, passengers, and cargo to the ocean's floor. Noah spotted yellowtail snapper and queen trigger fish darting around the wreckage.

He touched the edge of the hole and felt the rough metal. The ship's steel hull proved no match against the dangers of the ocean. Noah shook his head. Sunken ships riddled the waters off the Florida coast, the victims of reefs, hurricanes, and other storms.

A huge fish suddenly slid from the hull, his sharp white teeth smiling at Noah. Noah jerked backwards, pressing himself against the side of the ship. He dropped the piece of porcelain he'd been carrying and it sank into the sand below. His heart pounded in his chest. He worked to keep his breathing even and slow. The fish, a black-tip shark, swam leisurely past him. Although that species rarely hurt human beings, Noah wasn't taking any chances. He waited, moving as little as possible, until the shark faded into the murky distance.

Noah turned and gazed through the hole again. Did that shark have any companions?

Something grabbed Noah's shoulder, startling him again. His arms tingled with fear for an instant as he whirled around. What kind of fish was attacking him? With relief, he stared into his father's face mask. Frank Winter's long arms and legs moved slowly. His short brown hair waved in the sea water as he stared at Noah.

Scared twice in just a few moments! Noah chuckled to himself.

Frank gestured at Noah to follow him. Noah could see the anger in his dad's blue eyes. He had wandered too far from his parents. Frank pointed up. Noah nodded. It was time to surface.

He followed his dad, kicking with his feet as they swam back to the bridge where his mom was waiting.

She tipped her head upward and they all slowly ascended toward the ocean's surface. As Noah rose, the water grew clearer and rays of sunlight danced around him. The *San Isabel* was a dark hulking pile of metal below him. Then Noah's head bobbed into the open air. He slid his mask onto his forehead and pulled the regulator from his mouth. He sucked in a few breaths and smiled. What an adventure!

Noah's dad emerged beside him and Noah saw his frowning face.

"What were you doing so far away from us?" Frank scolded him.

"But Dad, you usually let me swim around the wreck without you," Noah said.

"I told you this time not to," Frank said.

"Why are you worrying about me?"

Frank took in a deep breath and let it out. "It's nothing, okay? But in the future, you need to listen to me."

"Yes, sir," Noah said.

Then his mom surfaced. She had a huge grin on her face.

"We found it!" she said as she held up something from the shipwreck.

CHAPTER TWO

NOT JUST ANY OLD SPYGLASS

"What is it?" Noah asked.

"Hold on." Riley tipped her head in the direction of the *Explorer*. "Time to get on board, then I'll tell you all about it."

Frank and Riley Winter were treasure hunters. They searched for items lost at sea. Sometimes, insurance companies hired the Winters to locate lost valuables, other times a collector would pay them to find some lost artifact. Treasure hunting involved not only diving shipwrecks, but also researching clues in old documents like ship logs, which detail the cargo and passengers aboard a ship, and journals from surviving passengers or crew members.

Noah and his parents paddled slowly over to the *Explorer*. By the time they got to the boat, Noah was breathing heavily.

"Good workout, right?" Frank said as he climbed the ladder into the boat and took off his diving tanks. Noah nodded as his dad helped him out of the water.

"Hey boss, how did it go?" said a tall, lanky young

man with dark hair and even darker eyes. Anthony Napolitano was the Winters' assistant. He was twenty-three years old and just out of college. He had helped Frank and Riley on expeditions since he was eighteen, working with them when he wasn't in school. Now that he'd graduated, he manned the boat and assisted with research. He also lived with the Winters and was like a big brother to Noah.

"Found the other piece," Riley answered as she got into the boat.

"Awesome!" Anthony said.

"Can I look at it?" Noah asked as he peeled off his mask.

"Be careful." Riley handed her prize to him. "Don't drop it."

Noah took the object from her. It was part of an old, brass spyglass, with two nested tubes, just like pirates used to use. Pieces of leather still covered part of the brass. He drew the spyglass out to its full length, about twelve inches.

"It's missing some tubing," Riley said, pointing at the tubes. "We found some of the other pieces a few days ago. A typical spyglass would have three or four tapering tubes that slide into each other, so it could be as long as twenty-five or thirty inches."

"It's sorta like the one I have at home." Noah put one end of the spyglass up to his eye and squinted into it, but all he saw was blue sky.

"Only yours is new." Riley held out a hand and Noah gave the spyglass back to her.

"If we can find the rest of the pieces, it should point us to the De La Rosa emerald," Frank said..

"How?" Noah asked.

"Get your gear off and I'll tell you," Frank smiled.

Riley handed the spyglass remnant to Frank. He carefully placed it in a felt-lined box where another brass piece lay.

Anthony helped Noah take off his regulator and oxygen tanks. "And what about you? Did you find anything?"

"Just part of an old flour sifter," Noah said as he slipped out of his diving suit. "But I dropped it when a shark came out of the hole in the ship."

Frank raised an eyebrow at his son. "What happened?"

"It's nothing," Noah said, then explained about the shark.

"You reacted well," Riley said. "Don't ever take a chance with a shark, even a smaller reef shark."

"Can't dive without running into a shark now and then." Anthony tousled Noah's bleach-blond hair.

"That's right," Frank said. "But you still need to be careful."

Noah nodded as he helped stow away his gear. Then he took a towel and dried himself off. As he did, he looked inside the box at the pieces of the spyglass his mom had found. It was somewhat worn, but in surprisingly good shape.

"How is this going to help us find the treasure?" Noah asked, once Frank and Riley had stripped off their gear. Frank and Anthony put the equipment away as Noah and his mom talked.

"The De La Rosa Emerald," Riley said with a smile. She wasn't much taller than Noah, who was almost five and a half feet tall. But Riley was lean and muscular from many years of swimming and diving. She toweled off her shoulder-length brown hair as she talked. "You know a little about the gem, right?"

Noah nodded.

"I know that Juan Carlo De La Rosa has hired us to find the De La Rosa Emerald that belonged to his ancestor, Roberto De La Rosa," Noah recited. "It's from Central America; it's shaped like a heart and supposed to be twice as big as a quarter."

"But gemstones are weighed in carats, which measures how big it is, so a gem that size would be..." Riley paused.

Quizzing Noah about the treasures was a game Frank and Riley liked to play.

"Somewhere around 120 carats," Noah completed Riley's statement. "And it would be worth at least a few million dollars today."

"And what happened to the jewel?" Riley kept quizzing him. "Do you remember?"

"In 1824, Roberto De La Rosa was going to return to Spain from the United States," Noah continued reciting the facts he'd memorized. "But, he worried that pirates would steal the jewel so before he went home to Spain, he hid it somewhere in the Florida Keys. He created a secret map so he could find the emerald when he came back. Only he never came back. The secret map was passed down through the De La Rosa family for a long time to, uh..."

"Alfonso De La Rosa," Frank said as he came back from the bridge. He sprawled on a cushioned bench. "In 1922, Alfonso sailed from Spain on the *San Isabel* to the United States, carrying the secret map with him, so he could find the hidden gem. But when the *San Isabel* sank, so did the spyglass."

"What happened to Alfonso De La Rosa?" Noah asked.

"He survived," Frank said. "But over time, the emerald was forgotten."

"Why?"

"Now that's a tale in itself," Riley said. As she talked, she frisked her hands through her hair to dry it. "Alfonso was obsessed with finding the emerald, so much so that he frequently neglected his family, including his son, Ernesto – "

"Who is Juan Carlo's grandfather," Anthony said as he returned from the cabin below.

"Right," Riley said. "So Alfonso journeyed to the

United States to search for the map spyglass that would then lead him to the emerald."

"But didn't they know that the ship sunk, and the spyglass with it?" Noah asked.

"Yes, but that's only part of the story. As your dad said, Alfonso survived the sinking, but he still was determined to find the spyglass. He searched the wreck site repeatedly. Keep in mind that, back in the 1920's and 30's, diving was without all the equipment we have now. It was very dangerous, and, sure enough, Alfonso died on one of those dives. Ernesto, his son, was so bitter about Alfonso's fatal fascination with the emerald that he vowed never to talk about it again," Riley continued. "And he kept that vow until he was an old man. Then, he began talking about the spyglass and the secret of the hidden emerald. He only told Juan Carlo about the spyglass a month ago."

"And Juan Carlo hired you to find it," Noah said.

"That's right. And you can help me with some research tomorrow, as part of your schoolwork," Riley said. Noah's mom homeschooled him, and whenever possible, she combined their current expedition work into Noah's studies.

Noah twisted his lip in thought. "So no one's found the emerald before because no one knew about it. Wow."

"Juan Carlo thinks the emerald is hidden somewhere on Key Largo," Anthony interjected.

"Yes," Frank answered. "That's what his grandfather Ernesto told him, but it's just a family rumor. And even if the rumor is correct, landmarks may change, so it could be impossible to locate with a map that's so old."

Noah sat down next to Frank and pointed to the spyglass pieces in the box. There was writing scrawled on the side of one of the tubes.

"What's this writing?" he asked.

"That's what told us we have the De La Rosa spyglass and not just any old spyglass," Riley said. "The maker of this special spyglass put his own name where a manufacturer's name usually would be."

"I don't understand how a spyglass will help us find the De La Rosa treasure," Noah said. "It's not a map."

"Ah, but it is! This spyglass was specially made by a man who worked for Roberto De La Rosa," Frank explained. "That's the maker's name on that piece," he said, pointing to the writing. "Roberto had the fellow design a spyglass with special end-pieces made of etched glass. Those pieces were attached to the end of the spyglass. You rotate the pieces a certain way, and the tubing extends to a specific length. If you do it exactly right and then shine a light through the spyglass, a map is projected out onto a flat surface, like a piece of paper or a wall."

"So what's missing? Do you need the other pieces

of tubing, and then you'll be able to see the map?" Noah asked.

"No, we have all the tubing pieces," Frank said. "What we're still missing are the glass end-pieces."

"They've got to be down there somewhere," Riley stared out into the water. "But that's only part of the hunt. Even if we can get the spyglass to project a map, we'll still have to decipher that map in order to find the emerald."

"You'll figure it out," Anthony grinned.

"Let's get back to shore," Frank said. "I want to examine the spyglass more closely."

"And," Riley turned back to them. "I think it's time to celebrate!"

Noah beamed.

"Celebrate what?" Frank asked, a twinkle in his eyes.

"Dad," Noah said, stretching out the word. "My birthday, remember?"

Frank frowned. "I wished you happy birthday this morning. Isn't that enough?"

Anthony laughed and poked Noah. "He's only kidding. Your mom's got cake and ice cream at home."

"What are we waiting for?" Noah said, pushing Anthony.

"Okay, okay." Anthony went aft and soon Noah heard the low groan of the *Explorer*'s engine. He sat back in a chair and looked around. There wasn't a cloud in the sky and the water shimmered like a yellow kaleidoscope, which reminded Noah of the spyglass. It was a perfect day to be out on the waters off Key West. Noah closed his eyes, letting the late afternoon sun warm him. He soon drifted off to sleep.

***

"Time to get up." His mom's voice called to him.

Noah opened his eyes and squinted. The *Explorer* was docked at the Sunset Marina and Frank and Anthony were securing her to the berth. Noah helped stow the diving gear inside the cabin. Then he followed the others up the pier to a green SUV parked in a lot nearby. After loading up some backpacks and a cooler, Frank drove them home.

The island of Key West is only two miles wide and four miles long. The Winters lived in Midtown, in a large house just a couple of blocks from the beach. The house was made of concrete cinder blocks and had numerous windows with wood blinds that let in the ocean breezes. Palm trees towered over the house, pool, and gardens where Riley liked to work.

"Take a quick shower and change for dinner," Riley instructed Noah as they entered the house from the garage.

Noah ran upstairs to the bathroom, stripped, and showered quickly. He could hardly wait for his birthday celebration. After he finished, he darted into his bedroom.

"Hey, Indy," Noah stopped to pet his cat, a calico named after Noah's favorite explorer, Indiana Jones. Noah had a *Raiders of the Lost Ark* movie poster on the wall, next to a map of the world. Pictures of Noah snorkeling and scuba diving sat on shelves hung over a small oak desk. The shelves also displayed some things Noah had found in his years of diving, like part of an old plate and a shark's tooth. Noah hoped to someday find a Spanish gold doubloon that he could put with his other treasures. The waters around Key West were filled with the doubloons, since many Spanish ships had wrecked there in centuries past.

"Here's what we're looking for," Noah said to Indy as he picked up a small spyglass from the desk. "Only mine's much newer."

Noah drew the spyglass out to its full length and peered out his window. Through the treetops, he could see the Gulf of Mexico.

"Noah!" he heard his mom's voice. "Come down for dinner."

"Coming!" Noah tossed the spyglass on the bed, startling Indy. "Sorry, Indy," he said as he raced out of the room.

Downstairs, his mom had set up dinner outside on the enclosed brick porch. They were having mangrove snapper that Frank had caught the day before, along with a salad and mashed potatoes. It was one of Noah's favorite meals.

"Okay, birthday boy," Frank smiled at him. "Chow down and then it's dessert."

***

"Let's open some presents and then have cake and ice cream," Riley said when they'd finished eating.

Noah grinned with delight as he untied a poster from Anthony. It was a painting of an old ship.

"The *Titanic*," Noah said, referring to the large passenger steamship that sunk in the North Atlantic in 1912, with the loss of 1,517 crew and passengers. Noah was fascinated with *Titanic* lore, but had never found a poster to put on the wall in his bedroom.

"Hope you enjoy looking at it every night," Anthony said.

"Thanks!" Noah studied the details of the ship. He was so excited he didn't think about a present from his parents.

"Hey, you're forgetting something," Riley said. She went into the house and returned with a long package wrapped in bright green paper.

"This is from your dad and me."

Noah tore off the paper, exposing a box with a spear gun inside. However, there were no spears with it.

"Wow!" He pointed it out into the garden. "This is cool."

"It's not a toy," Frank cautioned him. "We're going to keep the spears. We'll train you to use it properly, and you can use it only if your mom or I are with you."

"And it's to hunt fish that we'll eat," Riley said. "There's to be no killing just for sport."

"When can I go try it out?" Noah asked.

Riley leaned back in her chair. "You've got school tomorrow." Noah grimaced. "But if you get all your studies done without any fuss, we can go out in the afternoon."

"Thanks Mom!" Noah scooted away from the table. "May I go show this to Bradley?" Bradley, Noah's best friend, lived right down the street.

"Sure, but don't damage it. Clean up your plate and then you can go," Frank said.

Noah grabbed his plate and hurried into the kitchen.

"Be back by dark," Riley called to him.

"I will," Noah yelled as he ran out the front door.

CHAPTER THREE

MAX SCHEFF

Noah and Bradley had run through the neighborhood, pretending to hunt fish with his spear gun. Then they played basketball in Bradley's driveway. They felt perfectly safe because Chief Ben Burton, the Winters' next-door-neighbor, was also the Chief of Police for Key West.

Noah took a shortcut from Bradley's house and came through a gate into his backyard, walking past the pool and gardens. Dusk had fallen as he approached the house. His parents were sitting on the porch, talking in low voices.

"He shouldn't be out there," Riley said. "Not this time."

Noah stopped and listened.

"I don't know," Frank said. "He could help us search the debris field. The more people to look, the better chance we have to find the rest of the spyglass before someone else does."

They were talking about him! Noah tried not to make a sound. He tiptoed to the edge of the porch and peeked through the French doors. A breeze rustled through the garden and the palm trees swayed. Noah had to strain to hear his parents.

"It's not about that," Riley said. "If Max Scheff or someone else wants that emerald badly enough, Noah won't be safe."

Max Scheff! He was another treasure hunter who had interfered with some of the Winters' expeditions. On more than one occasion Noah's parents had raced to locate a valuable artifact before Max Scheff discovered it. He had even stolen a rare diamond from Noah's parents after they had found it.

"We've trained Noah to protect himself, in the water and on shore. He knows more than a lot of kids his age." Frank chuckled. "He could give James Bond a run for his money."

"He's still a boy."

"Are we overreacting?" Frank said. "We've been told to back off before."

"Not like this." There was an edge in Riley's voice. "That first letter was enough to scare me, but this one," Noah saw her lift a piece of paper off the table, then toss it toward Frank, "This one is even worse. No one has ever threatened to hurt us."

"That's true." Frank sighed. "When Juan Carlo asked us to help him find the emerald, I wondered if it was a bad idea. We're talking about an awful lot of money, the kind that would take care of our retirement.

Maybe we should stop now. But we sure could use the money from this expedition."

"I'll call Juan Carlo tomorrow," Riley said. "I'll tell him about the latest letter and see what he says. Maybe he can hire some other divers to help us."

"We need to find the emerald quickly and then we can move on. Anthony and I'll continue the search in the morning. Noah will have school, then you can take him out and show him how to use the spear gun. That'll keep him occupied so he won't be asking to help dive the wreck." Frank stood up and walked toward the French doors. "By the way, where is he?"

Noah jumped to action. He ran back past the pool and pretended to be just coming home.

"Hey, Dad," he said as Frank opened the door.

"Home in the nick of time," Frank said as Noah darted past him.

"Time for bed." Riley gave him a hug. "Was your thirteenth birthday fun?"

"Uh-huh," Noah said. "Bradley thinks the spear gun is cool."

"I'm glad you and Bradley like it." Riley and Frank followed him into the kitchen. "Off to bed. We'll see you in the morning."

Noah climbed the stairs to his bedroom. As he undressed, he thought about the conversation he'd overheard. Was Max trying to frighten his parents into quitting? And why would anyone want to hurt his parents? Noah didn't know his parents had been threatened before. But when valuables worth millions of dollars were in question, he guessed it made sense.

Noah crawled under the covers. Indy hopped onto the bed and curled up beside him.

"I'm sure they'll be fine," Noah whispered to Indy before he drifted off to sleep.

***

Wednesday morning, when Noah came downstairs, his dad and Anthony were already gone.

"Are they diving the wreck?" Noah asked, thinking about his parents' conversation the previous evening.

"Yes," Riley said. She noticed the crestfallen look on his face. "You've got schoolwork. But if you get all your exercises done, and you get at least eighty-five percent on your math test, then I'll teach you how to use the spear gun."

"All right!" Noah cheered.

He sat down at the kitchen table, wolfed down a bowl of cereal, then started on his schoolwork. He worked through some English and Spanish lessons, read some history, then took his math test right after lunch.

"Ninety percent on the nose," Riley said as Noah ate a cookie. "Great job." She showed him the incorrect questions and they worked through the errors.

"So do we get to go dive now? And learn how to use the spear gun?" Noah fired the questions at Riley.

Riley laughed. "Slow down. We've got a little

research to do on the *San Isabel*, and then we'll go out."

"Can we dive with Dad?"

Concern flashed across his mom's face, then disappeared. She shook her head. "He won't have time to come get us." Noah wondered about her worry. But before he could ask her anything, she spoke again. "Grab your pad and pencil and let's go into the living room."

Noah drug his feet as he tagged along with his mom.

"Don't be so disappointed," Riley said as she spread out a map on the coffee table. "We'll dive with your dad some other time."

She sat down on the couch and took a book from a stack on the floor next to the table. The Winters' living room looked like a museum. Bookshelves were filled with rare books and artifacts from their many dives.

"Now," Riley said as she opened the book. "One of the problems with finding the De La Rosa emerald is that Juan Carlo only knows what his grandfather told him. Supposedly, Alfonso carried the etched-glass pieces of the spyglass in a leather pouch in his pocket at all times. We know that Alfonso died while diving the wreck site. If the pouch was with him when he died, it's probably still somewhere in the debris field around the ship."

Noah knew that the debris field is the area around a shipwreck that contains the remains from the vessel. It could contain pieces of the ship itself, as well as items that people carried or the cargo the ship carried. Depending on the depth in which a ship sank, debris might be found miles from the wreckage itself.

"If we can figure out where Alfonso was last diving, that will at least give us a starting point to look for the glass end-pieces or the leather pouch, although I doubt the pouch survived in the salt water."

"How could we figure that out?"

"By looking through survivor accounts from the shipwreck," Riley said. "That might tell us if anyone was seen with the spyglass. I've also found some old articles about the sinking of the *San Isabel*, and some information about Alfonso, but I haven't had time to read them all. You can help with that while I read about the sinking of the ship."

"Sounds like searching for a needle in a haystack."

"Unfortunately that's true."

Riley stopped and cocked her head.

"What?" Noah asked.

"Sh." She held up a hand to silence him. They sat quietly for a moment. "Did you hear that?" Riley whispered.

Noah shook his head. Riley pushed herself gingerly off the couch and crept to the window. She peeked outside for a moment, her eyes scanning the backyard.

"I guess it was nothing," she said, coming back to the couch.

Noah eyed her carefully. Her hand shook slightly as she turned the pages of the book.

"Mom, what's wrong? Is someone after you?"

Riley stared at him. "Don't be silly, honey. It's nothing, just a little problem I'll be talking with Juan Carlo about tonight. Here." She handed him some papers. "Read through these and look for anything about Alfonso De La Rosa."

Noah finished in fifteen minutes. He flipped through the papers impatiently. He sighed loudly and kicked at the coffee table.

Riley, engrossed in her reading, didn't notice at first. Then she put a hand over his.

"How about this," she said, handing him another book. "This one should interest you."

"Why?"

"It's a new book about pirates." Riley pointed to the title. *Pirates and Treasure in Florida.* "This should interest you."

Noah reluctantly took the book from her. He started reading and was soon absorbed in the book. Reading about all the pirates who roamed southern Florida fascinated him. There were even pictures of their old spyglasses, which made Noah think about the De La Rosa spyglass.

After a while, Riley looked up. "Find out anything?"

Noah shook his head.

"I think it's time for a break. Go change and get your spear gun," she announced.

"All right!" Noah ran upstairs and changed into his swim trunks. He snatched the spear gun from the closet where he'd stored it the night before. "I get to use the gun!" he told Indy. The cat was sprawled out on the floor, in a square of sunlight streaming through the window. He opened one eye and stared at Noah, yawned, and went back to sleep. But Noah was already out the door.

***

"Here's how you load the gun." Riley took Noah's spear gun, placed the butt against her hip, and slid the blunt end of the spear shaft into the barrel of the gun. "You'll feel some resistance as you do this. Here, you try." Riley disengaged the safety, stuck the gun under the water and shot the spear into the sand. She grabbed the shot cord, which was attached to the spear and pulled the spear back to them.

They had driven east for a half hour on the Overseas Highway, the 127-mile, two-lane highway that ran the length of the Florida Keys, stopping at Ramrod Key. After parking, they'd grabbed their fins and snorkeling masks, and walked out to the beach. They waded out from shore and stood in a few feet of water. But Riley seemed distracted. She kept glancing over her shoulder and scanning the beach.

Noah took the gun from his mom, reengaged the

safety and loaded the spear. Then he shot it into the water and felt the jolt from the gun. "That's cool."

"Remember, it's not a toy. Never point the gun at people, even as a joke. Only spear fish you intend to eat. Now, the key to spearing a fish is to stalk the fish without spooking it," Riley said. "If you're diving, this can be difficult, but you're a good swimmer, so getting close without startling a fish shouldn't be a problem for you. You want to get within a few spear's lengths from the fish so the spear goes all the way through it. And always make sure there aren't any people where you're aiming."

"But we didn't bring any dive gear," Noah said. "Just our snorkeling masks and fins."

"We're just going to wade in the water today, so keep your net handy in case we spear something. I want you to get a feel for the gun. If you hit a fish, I'll help you kill it. Are you ready?"

Noah nodded his head eagerly. He loaded the gun again. They put on their fins and masks, then dove out into the warm water. Noah floated on the surface, paddling with his feet. He breathed through the snorkel and stared at the fish darting nearby. Riley swam beside him. After a few moments, Riley gestured at a large snapper. She made a motion for Noah to shoot the fish. Noah looked around. No one was in the water except them. He swam along with the fish, took deep breaths through his snorkel, and aimed the gun.

Swoosh! The spear zipped through the water, right past the fish. Noah looked at his mom. She was smiling as she snatched the cord and retrieved the spear. She came up to the surface by Noah.

"Not as easy as you would think, huh?" She handed him the spear.

Noah grimaced as he loaded the gun. "It's harder to load while I'm swimming," he gasped, spitting salty water out of his mouth.

"You'll get better at it."

Riley was right. After an hour, Noah could load the gun without much effort. But he was also tired from treading water so much.

"You want to take a break?" Riley asked.

"Uh-huh." Noah swam slowly back to shore, where he waited while Riley snorkeled for a little while longer. He lay down on his towel and daydreamed.

"Did you have a good time?" Riley asked as she strolled toward him a while later.

"Yeah, but I wish I'd caught a fish."

"Let's go home," Riley said as she toweled herself dry. "I'm sure you'll have better luck next time."

They took their gear and walked back to their car, a Honda Accord. After loading up, Noah slid into the passenger seat. "It was still fun."

Riley started the car and turned onto the Overseas Highway. Noah stared out at the turquoise water as she drove.

"Now what's he doing?" Riley broke the silence a few minutes later.

Noah glanced in the passenger door mirror. A large black SUV was pulling up close behind their car. The SUV was so close now that Noah noticed that the man in the passenger seat had spiked blond hair that almost looked white. His mom sped up but so did the SUV. Then Noah felt a terrifying jolt as the SUV rammed their car.

"What the…" Riley shouted as the car careened to the right. She jerked the wheel just before they hit the cement barrier on the side of the road.

The SUV backed off and then shot forward again. Metal crunched as the SUV crashed into the Honda. Noah slammed forward, his body jerking against the seatbelt. Riley screamed as she struggled to keep the car under control. A car horn honked as she swerved into the oncoming traffic lane.

"Mom, watch out!"

Riley cranked the wheel and the Honda veered back into the southbound lane. The SUV sped forward again, trying to ram their car. But the highway widened into four lanes and Riley slammed the gas pedal. The Honda zipped around a beat-up truck in front of them. Riley gripped the steering wheel so hard her knuckles turned white. Noah swiveled around and looked out the back of the car. The SUV tried to follow, but the truck blocked the way. The SUV lurched onto the oncoming traffic lane. Tires screeches as the SUV braked to a stop, cars careening around it. Riley sailed past two more cars, and they soon entered Key West.

Riley turned onto a side road and parked. Then she reached across and grabbed Noah's shoulder. "Are you okay?" she asked breathlessly.

Noah trembled but he couldn't find his voice.

"Hey." Riley put her arm around him. "It's okay."

Noah finally felt his body relax. "That was scary."

"I know." Riley took in a deep breath and let it out slowly. "Let's go." She drove down the street.

"Where are you going?" Noah asked, hearing the warble in his voice.

"To the harbor." Riley glanced in the rearview mirror. "Your father should be there by now."

In a few minutes, they pulled into the Sunset Marina parking lot.

"I see the *Explorer*," Noah yelled, waving at the boat. "Dad's back!"

"Let's go." Riley hurried out of the car.

Noah got out and ran with Riley down the dock. They jumped onto the *Explorer*.

"What's the matter?" Frank asked. He saw the fear on their faces.

"Noah, go sit inside," Riley instructed. Noah went into the bridge and peered out the window, watching his parents.

Riley gestured wildly as she relayed what had

happened. Frank kept glancing out at the parking lot as he listened. When Riley was finished, he wrapped her in a big hug. Noah crept to the door.

"…must know that we found the spyglass," Frank said.

"But we don't have the end-pieces," Riley said. "The spyglass is useless without those. They must know that."

"We need to talk to Juan Carlo. And we should tell Ben what happened," Frank said. "He should be at the station now."

They were going to talk to the chief of police! Noah thought.

Riley scanned the dock and parking lot. "It doesn't look like those men are coming here, at least not now, but what if they go to the house?"

Frank took in a deep breath and let it out slowly. "Let's see if Anthony can take Noah out to dinner and the arcade. We should be finished at the police station by then."

"I don't like this at all," Riley's voice shook.

"It'll be all right, I promise. How badly was the car damaged?" Frank asked.

"We came right here so I didn't even look."

"Let's check it out." Frank turned to the cabin and saw Noah listening. "Caught you eavesdropping. Well, come on out."

Noah emerged sheepishly from the cabin. "Who

rammed us?"

"I'm not sure," Frank answered. He wrapped Noah in a hug. "I'm glad you're okay."

Noah nodded, then followed his mom.

"You know that a lot of the things we look for are extremely valuable, right?" his mom asked Noah as they walked to the car.

"Uh-huh."

"And there are a lot of artifact collectors who don't care if they break the law in order to get the item they want. There's a huge underground market for these valuables. Many unscrupulous collectors will pay huge sums of money for artifacts, and they're willing to break the law in order to get what they want."

"That's wrong."

"It may be wrong, but that's what sometimes happens," Anthony said as he joined them. "I like working for your parents because they don't associate with those types of people."

"Thank you, Anthony," Frank said. They had reached the Honda and stopped to examine it. The rear bumper was crushed in and the right taillight was broken. The right rear side was also smashed.

Anthony's eyes widened when he saw the damage. "Wow, what happened?" Riley explained about the SUV. "That's not too bad, considering," Anthony said. "I'm glad they didn't hurt you."

"You can say that again," Frank said. He put his

arm around Noah.

"Would you mind taking Noah to dinner, and maybe the arcade, while we go talk to Ben Burton?" Riley asked Anthony.

"Sure," Anthony grinned. "I'll beat Noah at a game or two."

"In your dreams," Noah laughed.

"Take my car," Frank said, handing Anthony the keys to an SUV similar to the one that hit the Honda. "I'll ride with Riley."

"Come on," Anthony tugged Noah's arm. "We'll go to Big John's Pizza."

Big John's was Noah's favorite place to eat. "All right!" he said.

"We'll call when we're finished at the station," Frank yelled after them.

Noah didn't notice the worried look on his mother's face as he and Anthony got in the SUV and drove off.

***

A few hours later, Noah and Anthony had just completed an intense game of video boxing when Anthony pulled his cell phone from his pocket.

"That's strange," he said. "Your dad hasn't called yet."

"Maybe they're still talking to Chief Burton," Noah said, feeding another quarter into the game.

Anthony dialed the phone. After a few moments,

he hung up, his eyebrows scrunched up. "No answer." He started to walk away.

"Hey, wait." Noah gestured at the video game. "One more game?"

Anthony came back. "Okay." But Noah could tell that Anthony was distracted. Noah beat him easily, which was usually not the case.

"We should go now," Anthony said.

Noah followed Anthony out of Big John's. They drove home in silence. When Anthony turned onto their street, he slowed before arriving at the house.

"Are those men in the SUV back?" Noah asked.

Anthony scanned the street, then the front of the house. The sun was low on the horizon and the house was bathed in deep shadows. No lights were on in the house.

"I guess they're not home yet," Anthony said.

Noah nodded. His heart fluttered. Anthony's anxiety was rubbing off on him.

Anthony parked in the driveway. They got out and slowly approached the front porch. Indy leaped out of the bushes. Noah and Anthony jumped.

"It's just the cat," Anthony said, the tension broken. "Your parents must have gone for a bite to eat." He took out his key and unlocked the door.

"Indy," Noah picked up the cat. "What are you doing out here?"

Anthony opened the door and turned on the living

room light.

"Whoa…" Noah said, his voice trailing off. They both stared inside.

The house had been ransacked.

CHAPTER FOUR

SPIKE MAN

Noah gaped at books and papers, scattered everywhere. The cushions on the couch were ripped open, and stuffing was strewn about. All the contents of the bookshelves had been swept onto the floor. Noah set Indy down. The cat growled, then skittered upstairs, his tail puffed out.

"Let's see if Chief Burton's home." Anthony backed out of the house, dragging Noah with him.

"Mom and Dad must be with Chief Burton." Noah's voice shook. "They must have come home, seen this and went to report it."

"Your parents are fine," Anthony reassured Noah as they cut across Chief Burton's lawn to his front door. Anthony rapped on the door. A moment later, Chief Burton appeared.

"Hey Anthony, Noah," Chief Burton smiled. He was an ex-football linebacker who had played for Florida State. Ben was tall and bulky, with big hands and a thick neck, but thin hair. "What can I do for you?"

"Well, sir," Anthony began.

"Have you seen my parents?" Noah blurted out. "We haven't seen them and someone broke into the house!"

"What?" Chief Burton gazed at them for a second. "Hold on." He dashed into his home office. Noah heard a closet door open and shut, then Chief Burton appeared with a gun in his hand.

"Stay here," Chief Burton ordered them.

Noah and Anthony waited in Chief Burton's entryway while he sprinted across the lawn and into the Winter house.

"But what about Mom and Dad?" Noah asked. His stomach knotted up with worry.

"They're fine," Anthony reassured him again.

They waited agonizing minutes while Chief Burton was gone. Then he materialized out of the darkness. He was talking on his cell phone.

"The house is empty," he said as he brushed past them and into his office. He hung up the phone. "Come in here and sit down."

Noah and Anthony sat down on a leather couch across from him.

"Frank and Riley left the station a couple of hours ago," Chief Burton said as he sat down behind the desk and picked up a notepad. He focused on Noah. "I want you to tell me everything you can about that SUV that rammed your car earlier today."

Noah's mouth went dry. This was serious. "It

happened so fast," he began, then related everything he could remember.

"Did your mom say anything about recognizing them?" Chief Burton asked when he'd finished. Noah shook his head. "Did you see the men?"

Noah screwed up his lip, thinking. "The passenger had spiked blond hair, but I couldn't see the driver." Outside the window, Noah spied blue and red lights flashing. The police had arrived at his house.

"That helps," Chief Burton said, jotting down everything Noah said. He turned to Anthony. "Do you remember Riley or Frank talking about anyone threatening them?"

"Frank said he wondered if Juan Carlo knew of anyone who was trying to beat him to the treasure," Anthony said.

"Juan Carlo?" Chief Burton asked.

"Juan Carlo De La Rosa is the one who hired the Winters to find the De La Rosa emerald."

Chief Burton nodded. His cell phone rang. "Yeah?" he answered. "Okay, be right over."

He set down the phone and eyed Noah. He tapped on the desk, gathering his thoughts. "Noah, I don't know where your parents are."

Noah's lower lip trembled but he told himself to be strong. He'd heard his parents talk about the dangers of their work. But it was still hard to hear it.

"We're putting out an APB, an all-points-bulletin,

for them," Chief Burton said. "The police all over the state will be looking for them. Hopefully your parents are out searching for the emerald and they don't know about the house being torn up."

"But they would've called," Noah said.

Chief Burton frowned. "I know, son. But I've got my men dusting for fingerprints and looking for clues to help us find who ransacked the house. When they're done, you two can go home."

"But what if whoever did this comes back?" Noah asked.

"I know you're scared," Chief Burton said. "But we'll keep you safe. We've checked the entire house and property to make sure no one's around. The police will be watching the house all night, and I'll be watching, too, so you won't be in any danger."

"Sir, may I have a word with you?" Anthony asked Chief Burton.

"Sure." Chief Burton and Anthony went into the kitchen. Noah could hear their voices, low murmurs, as they talked. But he was thinking about his parents. Were they okay? Were they in an accident? Did they go look for the emerald and forget to call Anthony and tell him? That didn't seem like them, but when his parents got excited, Noah knew they could forget about other things. His palms grew sweaty. "They're fine," he told himself. He wiped his palms on his shorts and tried to keep his fear at bay.

"You can stay here until we're done at your house," Chief Burton said as he and Anthony came back into the office.

"Thanks," Noah said automatically.

Chief Burton left the house. Anthony sat down beside Noah.

"It's going to be okay," he said.

Noah stared at the floor. "What do you think happened?"

"I don't know," Anthony replied. "But when we get back in the house, we're going to do everything we can to find your parents."

***

It was well past midnight by the time Noah and Anthony returned home. The house was still in disarray, only now, spots of powder marked the door handles and window frames where the police had dusted for fingerprints. Noah glanced around at the mess.

"What do we do?" he asked.

Anthony ran a hand through his curly hair. "We need to call Juan Carlo. He might know who else is after that emerald."

"They might hurt my parents to get information about the emerald." Noah shuddered to think what that might mean.

"Yes. But don't worry, your parents are smart. They won't get hurt."

They went into Frank's office. Pictures of Riley,

Frank, and Noah diving were on the floor, the glass broken. Books were strewn about. The computer was on, showing the log-on screen.

"I kept telling Frank not to give me his password," Anthony said as he sat down and logged into the computer. "But now I'm glad he did."

Anthony found Juan Carlo's phone number. "I'll put it on speaker," he said as he dialed the number.

The sound of a phone ringing filled the room.

"Hello?" a sleepy voice said.

"Juan Carlo? It's Anthony Napolitano."

"Hola, my friend." Juan Carlo spoke in a deep, accented voice. "How are you and the Winters? It is very late. Is something wrong?"

Anthony glanced at Noah. "Something happened to Riley and Frank." Anthony explained all that had transpired. Juan Carlo didn't say a word until Anthony finished.

"This is very bad," Juan Carlo said. "Noah, I am sure your parents are fine. They are strong people."

"Yes, sir," Noah replied, trying to sound confident.

"I will fly down there immediately," Juan Carlo said. "We must find Riley and Frank as soon as possible."

"The police put out an APB," Anthony said.

"Ah, that is good," Juan Carlo said. "But not enough. I will make arrangements as soon as I hang up. I will be there early in the morning. Then we will resolve this."

"Thanks," Anthony said, and hung up.

Noah started straightening the office.

"Why don't you go to bed," Anthony suggested. "We can deal with this in the morning."

"I'm not tired," Noah said.

Anthony shrugged. Then he bolted out of his chair. "The *Explorer*! Did those men try to get to the boat?"

"That's where the brass pieces of spyglass are?"

Anthony nodded. "Frank took the spyglass tubes with him this morning. He locked them in the safe on the *Explorer* while we dove the wreck."

"Unless Mom and Dad went back to the boat while we went to dinner, the spyglass should still be there," Noah said.

They ran out of the house and to the truck.

"We need to get those spyglass pieces," Anthony said as he started the engine.

On a small island like Key West, it only took a couple of minutes to drive to the harbor.

"You better stay here," Anthony said as he parked the SUV. "Phil's not a nice guy and he'll wonder why a kid is out after midnight." Phil Harris, the night watchman, was a cranky old man who adhered to the rules no matter what.

Noah nodded, secretly wishing he could go with Anthony. He scrunched low in his seat so Phil couldn't see him, but left the window down and watched as

Anthony ran up to the harbor office. Noah saw Phil come to the door.

"Anthony, what are you doing here?" Noah heard Phil's booming voice.

"Sorry to bother you, but I need to get into the *Explorer*."

Phil eyed Anthony. "Harbor's not open."

"It's an emergency," Anthony pleaded.

Phil shook his head. "Nope. I've had other riffraff coming around here, and now you. I've had to do extra patrols on the wharf because of that. Now go on."

As he came back to the truck, Anthony's mouth was twisted into an angry scowl. "Sounds like those men already tried to get past Phil. We've got to check the boat."

"There's a hole in the fence, down on the edge of the property," Noah said, pointing.

"I like the way you think," Anthony grinned. He started the car and drove out of the parking lot. A moment later, he parked on a side street.

"Show me where the hole is." Anthony grabbed a small flashlight out of the glove compartment. Noah got out and quietly shut his door.

They scurried across the street, then crouched low and darted along the high chain-link fence that ran from the edge of the property down into the water, enclosing the wharf.

"Here it is," Noah whispered. A portion of the

fence was pulled away from the ground.

Anthony got down on his hands and knees. "I don't think I can fit." He tugged at the fencing. It rattled loudly in the darkness.

"Sh!" Noah hissed. He squatted down and pushed Anthony out of the way. "I'll go."

"You can't!" Anthony tugged at Noah's leg.

"We can't waste any time." Noah squiggled through the hole. "I know everything about that boat and the harbor. I'll be fine." He took the flashlight from Anthony.

"Be careful," Anthony whispered. "If you're not back in ten minutes, I'm going to Chief Burton."

Noah ducked down and ran to the dock, making his way past a variety of boats. The moon shone like a spotlight in the sky and tinted everything with an eerie glow. Noah stopped near the *Explorer* and caught his breath. The *Explorer* bobbed gently with the waves. Inside was dark. She looked okay.

Noah stepped across the gap between the boat and wharf, onto the *Explorer*. He waited a moment and listened. He heard waves lapping against the boat, but nothing else. He went to the cabin door, unlocked it, and stepped into the cabin. He stared into the deep shadows. The room appeared undisturbed. He took the flashlight, covered the end with his hand so the beam wouldn't glow as brightly, then shone it around. Nothing seemed out of place.

Noah crossed to a set of cabinets, bent down and slid open a door. A small gray safe sat inside. It did not appear to have been tampered with. Noah reached for the lock but stopped. Was that a noise? He quickly turned off the flashlight. He paused and listened. His breathing sounded loud in the darkness. Noah cranked his head around but saw nothing out the windows.

"My imagination," he muttered to himself.

He turned the flashlight back on, taking a risk as to whether Phil was patrolling around the *Explorer*. He held the flashlight with his mouth, shining the light on the safe. He twisted the dial back and forth, and unlocked the safe. He opened the door. The box his dad used to store small artifacts sat there. Noah opened it. Inside, two pieces of brass spyglass shone dully in the flashlight's beam.

Noah let out a sigh of relief. "They didn't move it."

He picked up the box, then noticed a notebook underneath it. His dad's notes! *Good thing that wasn't at the house,* he thought. Noah grabbed it and closed the door of the safe. He stood up and froze.

This time he was sure he heard something.

He shut off the flashlight and ducked down. Thump! Noah sank to his knees. Someone was trying to get on the boat. Noah held his breath, then peeked out through a side window. He scanned the inky black water off the port side. In the moonlight, he saw a head and then arms clutching at an aluminum ladder that had been thrown over the side of the boat. A man in a wet suit emerged from the water. He pulled his mask up over his forehead. Noah gasped. It was the man with the spiked blond hair.

Noah thought fast. He crawled on his knees to the door, reached up and gently turned the knob. He edged the door open and peeked out. The man hadn't made it up the ladder yet.

Noah dashed out the door and ran to the other side of the boat. He leaped onto the dock, praying that Phil, or the spiked blond man's companion, wasn't around. He landed hard, his feet smacking the ground, but he didn't care. He ran past other boats, not looking behind him. In a few moments, he returned to the hole in the fence.

"What's wrong?" Anthony whispered.

Noah pushed the box and notebook under the fence, then crawled through. He got to his knees, wheezing.

"What's wrong?" Anthony repeated.

"Spike Man," Noah panted.

"What?" Anthony looked bewildered.

Noah glanced over his shoulder. No one was following him. "Get to the car." He prodded Anthony. They grabbed the box and Frank's notebook and ran back to the truck.

Once inside, Noah breathlessly told Anthony about

Spike Man.

"They're after the spyglass," Anthony said through gritted teeth. He wasted no time leaving the area. "Good thing we beat them to it. We have to watch our step."

A few minutes later as they drove down their street, a patrol car passed them.

"The police are keeping an eye out," Noah said.

They went into the house. Anthony made sure all the doors and windows were securely locked.

"I'll keep this with me," Anthony held up the box and Frank's notebook.

Noah nodded, stifling a yawn.

"Time for you to hit the hay," Anthony said.

Noah protested. In truth, he was worried sick, but he could feel sleep tugging at him. He started up the stairs, but stopped. What if someone was up there?

Anthony must have sensed his fear. "Come on, let's go check your room." He climbed the stairs after Noah. "I know the police have been through the house, but until I check myself, my mind says it's not safe."

Noah nodded gratefully, glad Anthony was with him. They entered Noah's room. The intruders had turned it upside down, even tearing his new *Titanic* poster. Noah picked it up.

"That stinks," Anthony said angrily. Then he patted Noah's shoulder. "We'll get you another one." He went over and remade the bed. "Here, good as new. See, Indy's ready for bed." The cat appeared from under the bed.

"Thanks, Anthony," Noah said to his friend.

Anthony smiled at him. "You get some sleep. We'll figure this out in the morning, and before you know it, your parents will be home." He left the room with the box and notebook under his arm.

Noah stared at the disarray in his own room. As he crawled into bed, anger replaced fear. If someone hurt his parents, they would be sorry. He gazed into the darkness for a long time before sleep finally overtook him.

CHAPTER FIVE

ISLAND OF THE BARRACUDAS

Noah rushed downstairs the next morning, hoping his parents had returned during the night. But when he came into the kitchen, instead of his parents, Anthony was sitting at the table, drinking coffee with a small man with hair as dark as coal.

"Look who's up," Anthony said. "Noah, meet Juan Carlo."

Juan Carlo stood up. He was not much taller than Noah. Juan Carlo wore a dark blue suit with a yellow tie. He shook Noah's hand firmly.

"I am pleased to meet the son of Frank and Riley," Juan Carlo spoke very formally, his accent thick.

"Hi," Noah said glumly.

"You okay?" Anthony asked.

Noah shrugged. All he could think about was his parents. Were they okay? Tears welled up in his eyes. He hurriedly brushed them away.

Anthony came over and hugged him. "Hey, I know you're worried," Anthony said. "But we'll find your parents."

"How?" Noah asked.

"We're going to figure out where your parents are," Juan Carlo said. He had a neatly trimmed mustache that he smoothed with his fingers. "The question, as you say, is how. You know nothing of these men that hit your car?" he asked Noah.

Noah shook his head. "I only saw the passenger, but I've never seen him before. He has spiked blond hair."

Juan Carlo pursed his lips. "This is bad."

"What?" Anthony and Noah said at the same time.

"That man is Dave 'The Wrench' Dixon. He works for Max Scheff."

Noah frowned. Max Scheff hired out himself to the highest bidder and he stopped at nothing to get what he wanted.

"Dave 'The Wrench'," Anthony said as he sat back down at the table. "His weapon of choice is a wrench, huh."

Juan Carlo nodded.

"This is bad," Noah echoed Juan Carlo's sentiment.

Juan Carlo nodded again. "Sí, Max must have kidnapped your parents, Noah."

"What will this guy do to my parents?" Noah's voice shook.

"Mark my words, he will exchange your parents for the map." Juan Carlo gripped Noah's arm. "Max will not let Dave hurt your parents. Max wants the map, that's all."

"But we don't have the map at all," Anthony said. "We only have the spyglass, not the pieces of glass with the map etched on them."

"And there is also a third piece that attaches to the etched pieces of glass. It has lines to mark the exact spot to look," Juan Carlo said.

"X marks the spot," Noah tried to smile.

"Yes," Juan Carlo said. "But I could never picture exactly how it all fit together to make a treasure map."

"We may never find any of it," Anthony moaned. "If Alfonso had them with him when he died, they could be anywhere around the shipwreck."

"Ah, I think I can help with that," Juan Carlo said. His dark eyes twinkled. He opened a briefcase sitting on the table and drew out something wrapped in cloth. He unfolded the cloth, exposing an old leather-bound book. "This should help."

"What is it?" Noah asked.

"It's a journal that my great-grandfather, Alfonso, kept. In it, he tells where he hid the glass pieces for the spyglass."

"What?" Anthony bolted upright. "But I thought Alfonso kept the pieces with him at all times."

Juan Carlo chuckled. "That was true, until after he survived the shipwreck. When Alfonso began searching the shipwreck for the spyglass tubes, he realized that he might lose the glass pieces if he carried them with him when he was diving. So he hid them." Juan Carlo put his hand on the journal. "This tells us where."

"Why didn't you tell my parents?" Noah asked.

"I had to be very careful with this information. If someone else recovered the rest of the spyglass, I didn't want him to know how to find the glass pieces. That emerald belongs to my family."

"So once you knew Frank and Riley had the spyglass, then you would tell them," Anthony said.

"Exactly." Juan Carlo scowled. "They were successful, but now they are in danger."

"Where does the journal say the etched pieces are hidden?" Noah asked.

"I know this by heart, but I will show you." Juan Carlo carefully opened the Alfonso's journal. Elegant, faded handwriting filled the sheets. He gingerly leafed through each page. "This is a part of my history. My great-grandfather's notes here said that he hid a steel box of valuables, including the glass pieces, in 'The Island of the Barracudas'. So we go to that island, and we find the box."

"I've never heard of it," Anthony said.

Juan Carlo's face fell. "You don't know this island?"

Anthony shook his head. "But I've only lived here for a few years."

"I've never heard of it either," Noah said.

"Where's the best place to get maps of the Keys?"

"Let's go to the library," Noah said. "They've got a Florida History section, with some books about the history of the Keys that are way better than anything on the Internet."

"How do you know this?" Juan Carlo asked.

Noah smiled shyly. "Mom makes me learn about the Florida Keys for school. And it helps her and Dad with treasure hunting."

Juan Carlo wrapped up the journal and put it back in his briefcase. "Very good. Let us get started."

Noah ate a quick breakfast and was putting on his shoes when the phone rang.

"Hello?" he said.

"Is this Noah Winter?" The voice sounded muffled.

"Yes."

"We have your parents." Noah clearly heard the menace in the voice.

"Where are they? Who is this?" He hit a button on the phone, turning on the speakerphone. Anthony and Juan Carlo came over. "Who is it?" Anthony mouthed at Noah. Noah shrugged.

"Who is not important. We want the spyglass. Bring it to us and we'll let your parents go unharmed."

Noah blanched. Sure enough, his parents had been abducted! He opened his mouth but no words came out.

"We don't have the entire spyglass," Anthony said.

There was a pause. "You are the Winters' assistant. I'm sure you're capable of finding all the pieces. We'll call back in twenty-four hours, at noon tomorrow, with directions on where to leave the spyglass."

"We can't possibly deliver it by then," Anthony said.

"Then the boy's parents will meet an unfortunate accident," the voice said.

"That's not enough time," Noah cried.

"I wouldn't waste a minute, then." Click. The dial tone echoed loudly in the kitchen.

Noah slumped against the wall. "My parents…we have to help them."

"We can only do that by delivering the spyglass with the map," Anthony said.

"Then we have to find those glass end-pieces!" Noah nearly shouted.

"Come, come." Juan Carlo grabbed Noah's shaking shoulders. "You must be strong. We will find the glass pieces with your help."

"You're right," Noah said, summoning up all the courage he could. "I learned a lot about treasure hunting from Mom and Dad. I know we can find them."

"I'll call Chief Burton and tell him about the call," Anthony said.

"Where is Frank's notebook?" Juan Carlo asked. "I'll look through that and see if there is anything that will help us."

Anthony left and returned a minute later with the notebook. Then he called Chief Burton.

Noah paced the kitchen while Anthony talked to Chief Burton. Juan Carlo sat at the table with the notebook.

"He's sending a detective over," Anthony said when he hung up.

They sat at the table as silent minutes ticked by. Noah rested his head on his arms, a helpless feeling washing over him. Were his parents okay?

Anthony stared out the window. Juan Carlo flipped through Frank's notes and sipped coffee.

"What is this about a 4x4?" Juan Carlo asked a few minutes later.

"A 4-wheel drive vehicle," Anthony replied. "Like a truck or a Jeep."

Noah raised his head. "What did you say?"

"He was asking about a truck," Anthony said.

Noah turned to Juan Carlo. "You said four by four."

"Sí," Juan Carlo said.

"That's in Dad's notes?" Noah continued.

Juan Carlo pushed the notes to Noah. "Sí, right there." He pointed.

Frank had scribbled "4x4 – check" on the page.

"What is it?" Anthony asked.

"4x4 is the nickname Dad gave a cave that he explored a long time ago," Noah said. "He said the cave entrance was so small, it's four inches by four inches." Anthony and Juan Carlo gazed at him with blank looks on their faces. "It was a joke. A 4x4 truck is big. Dad was joking that the entrance was just the opposite."

"Oh," Juan Carlo said, still looking confused.

Anthony grabbed the notes. "Where is the cave?"

Noah shrugged. "I just heard Dad say '4x4'. I don't know the real name for the place. I don't think he wanted me to know, maybe because I can't dive in underwater caves until I'm fifteen and can get certified. Dad said it's a dangerous place to dive or snorkel because of the currents and the reefs. I don't think too many people go there."

"A perfect place for Alfonso to have hidden some-thing," Juan Carlo said.

"But where is it?" Anthony said with frustration.

"I will bet that if we figure out where the 'Island of the Barracudas' is, we'll find that '4x4' cave," Juan Carlo said.

The doorbell rang, interrupting their conversation. Anthony left the room, returning a moment later with a tall, wiry man.

"This is Detective Shaw," Anthony said.

Shaw put his hand to his forehead in an informal salute, then leaned against the countertop and flipped open a tiny notepad.

"I need you to relate the entire phone call," he said brusquely. His short haircut, beady eyes, and big nose didn't make for a very friendly impression.

"It's not much," Noah said. He described the call. Anthony and Juan Carlo agreed that he had the details correct.

"We'll see if we can trace the call but I doubt we'll find anything. The man knew to keep the call short, and he probably used a cell phone with a temporary number. He's too smart to let a call be traced back to him. But we'll set things up to monitor the next call, just in case." Shaw got up and shook their hands. "Chief Burton or I will keep in touch. You all need to be extra careful."

"We can't possibly run into trouble at the library," Noah said after Shaw left.

Noah was correct about that. But their quest to find Noah's parents had just begun. And trouble *did* follow.

CHAPTER SIX

COPPER KEY

The Key West Library is a small white building on Fleming Street. Along with its many books, outside there is a palm garden with tropical foliage from around the world. Some days when Noah visited the library, he would sit in the garden and work on his school studies. But today he was focused on one thing only: locating the 'Island of the Barracudas'.

"They have some old maps," Noah said, once they were in the Florida History section. "Maybe some of them show an 'Island of the Barracudas'."

"Good idea," Anthony said.

But after checking numerous maps, they still had not found the island.

"This is no good," Juan Carlo said, rubbing his mustache.

Noah walked along the bookshelves and perused titles. "Here." He started pulling some books off the shelves. "I've read parts of these. I know they talk about the history of the Keys."

"Then we'll check them," Anthony said, taking a

book and sitting down.

Noah brought more books to the table and began reading. They turned pages in silence. As time flew by, Noah grew more concerned. He kept glancing at a clock on the wall above the door. He finally slammed his book closed.

"We've been at this for more than an hour and haven't found anything about Barracuda Island. And look at all the books that are left. This is taking too long."

"I know," Juan Carlo said. "But we have to keep looking."

Noah shook his head in frustration. "I've got a better idea." He had noticed that Mrs. Turner, the elderly librarian, had returned from lunch. He waited while she helped another patron, then walked quietly up to her desk.

"Hi, Mrs. Turner, I was wondering if you could help me with something."

"Hello, Noah," Mrs. Turner smiled at him. "How are your folks?"

"They're just fine." Noah almost choked on the words. "Um, could I ask you a question?"

"That's one." Mrs. Turner laughed at her joke. "Of course you may."

"I'm trying to find out about a place around here that was called 'Island of the Barracudas'."

Mrs. Turner took off her reading glasses. "Now

that's a funny name. Are you sure you don't mean 'Key' instead of 'Island'?"

"It's possible. But there isn't a Barracuda Key either."

"You're right about that." Mrs. Turner primped her silver hair as she thought. "Your parents must be looking for treasure. Did you look in the Florida Keys section?"

"We're checking in there now," Noah said.

Mrs. Turner stood up. "There's one book that's a great resource. Let me look it up." She typed for a moment, then wrote something down. "Let's see if this book will help."

Noah followed her back into the Florida Keys section. Mrs. Turner scanned the shelves, then pulled out a book. "Let's look in this one." She opened it and flipped through pages, muttering to herself. "Hm. Nothing here on 'Island of the Barracudas'."

She put the book back and slowly walked along the shelves, periodically pulling a book out. She would quickly scan it and then put it back. Noah fidgeted impatiently.

"I'm just not finding anything," Mrs. Turner said. "You've looked at the maps?"

"Yes," Noah said. "None of them show an 'Island of the Barracudas'."

Mrs. Turner thought some more but shook her head. "I don't know then. I wish I could be of more help."

"Thanks, anyway." Noah walked away, his shoulders drooping.

"Wait," Mrs. Turner said.

Noah whirled around.

"I have an idea," she continued. "There's an old man who lives on Stock Island. James River is his name. He's somewhat of a history buff about the Keys. He comes around here once in a while, although I haven't seen him in a month or so. If anyone would know of a place around here called Island of the Barracudas, it would be him."

Noah brightened. "Do you have his number?"

"He doesn't have a phone," Mrs. Turner said. "He doesn't like them. You'll have to drop by his house." She wrote down his address.

"Thanks so much." Noah hurried back to Anthony and Juan Carlo.

"I heard," Anthony murmured to Noah. He was already getting the SUV keys out. "Good idea asking her. Let's go."

Stock Island was immediately east of Key West. They drove the Overseas Highway, jammed with cars headed to Key West for the weekend, and crossed to Stock Island.

James River lived in a small house on 11th Avenue. The front yard was enclosed in a pink cinderblock fence. The tiny lawn seemed no bigger than a sandbox. Noah, Anthony, and Juan Carlo let themselves in the metal gate and went to the front door. Noah rang the bell.

After a few minutes, Noah sighed. "Shoot, he's not home. Maybe a neighbor is around." He started for the gate, then halted when he heard singing coming from the back yard.

"Come on." Anthony and Juan Carlo followed Noah around the side of the house. He heard the song more clearly. It was "Amazing Grace". He'd heard it in church many times.

A tall, slender dark-skinned woman was picking mandarin oranges off a tree in the center of the yard. Her shoulder-length, straight hair swirled slightly when she turned toward Noah, and her large hazel eyes sparkled. She kept singing. She looked like she was in her early twenties, and Noah thought she was beautiful.

"Excuse me?" Noah cleared his throat nervously.

"Yes?"

"I, uh, we," Noah gestured at Anthony and Juan Carlo, "Uh, we're looking for James River."

The woman blinked a couple of times, sadness flooding her eyes. "Oh, honey, I'm sorry to say that he passed on a few weeks ago."

Noah's heart leaped into his throat. "I'm sorry to hear that." He really was sorry the old man had died. But he also wondered if his chance of finding 'Island of the Barracudas' was gone, too.

"I'm his granddaughter, Deidra." She set the oranges in her basket, reached out and shook Noah's hand. "Is there something I can help you with?"

"Mrs. Turner, at the library in Key West, told us that Mr. River was a historian of the Keys. We were hoping he could tell us about an island around here that was called 'Island of the Barracudas'."

"Hm. I've never heard of that one." Deidra picked up the basket. "Let's go in the house. I'm a graduate student myself, studying Florida history, so I've read through a lot of Poppy's books and notes."

"You like history, like your grandfather?" Noah asked.

"It's in the blood." Deidra opened the back door and let them in the house. A ceiling fan lightly stirred the hot, humid air. She set the basket down and wiped her hands on a dish towel. "Poppy had a few old books about the Keys. Let's look in them."

Noah looked hopefully at Anthony and Juan Carlo.

They followed Deidra into the living room. One entire wall was filled with bookcases. Deidra stooped down, where worn volumes of books were laid. She ran a hand along the spines, reading titles.

"I don't know which books would be the best." She made a 'tsk' sound. "They're quite old and Poppy didn't take care of them very well. He should've gotten them out of this humidity."

"Knock, knock," a voice called, and the front screen door rattled.

Deidra stood up. "Mr. Thorndike, come on in."

A wizened old man let himself in. "Hello Miss Deidra. How y'all doing today?"

"Fine, thank you. Just cleaning some things up in Poppy's yard."

The old man eyed the strangers.

"Mr. Thorndike, I'd like you to meet Noah, Anthony, and Juan Carlo," Deidra introduced them. "They came here hoping to ask Poppy some questions about the Keys."

"I see," Mr. Thorndike said. "James and I spent a lot of years around these Keys, hee-hee. I expect I'm about as old as the Keys myself."

"Maybe you know the place they're looking for," Deidra said. "The Island of the Barracudas?"

"Island of the Barracudas." Mr. Thorndike rubbed at his gray beard stubble. "Now that takes me back. I seem to recall that folks used to call Copper Key that. 'Cause of all the barracudas around it." He winked at Noah.

"Really?" Noah perked up. "Are you sure Copper Key is it?"

Mr. Thorndike nodded slowly. "I believe so. They say a long time ago pirates gave it that name."

Noah stared at him, eyes wide. "Are there really barracudas there?"

"Not anymore," Mr. Thorndike laughed. "At least not that I've heard."

"Is there a cave on Copper Key as well?" Anthony

asked. "One that's hard to dive because of the currents?"

"Yes, sir." Mr. Thorndike answered. "I've heard about that cave. Supposed to be on the north side. But you can't go there. That Key is owned by Isaiah Wright. There's no way he'll let you on the island."

"I've heard of him," Noah said, remembering things he'd heard from his parents.

Isaiah Wright was a recluse who had lived on Copper Key for over fifty years. He rarely left the island, where he had a full staff of house servants to take care of him, and he closely guarded his privacy. Boats patrolled the waters around the Key and sentries watched the boat dock twenty-four hours a day to keep strangers out. Wright himself was an expert marksman, and had been known to shoot at unwanted 'guests'.

"Thank you for the information." Juan Carlo reached out and shook Mr. Thorndike's hand.

"You've been very helpful," Deidra patted Mr. Thorndike on the shoulder. "I don't know if we would've found that in any of Poppy's books."

Noah looked at the books on the shelves. After all that time they'd spent in the library, he was grateful for Mr. Thorndike's information. No more perusing books, at least for now.

"Should we tell Chief Burton about this?" Noah asked as they drove off.

Anthony shook his head. "If we do, who knows what the police will do. They could keep us from looking there ourselves and delay things."

"I think Anthony is right," Juan Carlo said. "We must find the chest with the etched-glass pieces ourselves. That is the best hope for your parents."

"Now I know why Dad didn't tell me about the 4x4 cave," Noah said. "He wasn't supposed to be diving there."

"And we aren't either," Anthony said. "But that's not going to stop us."

***

The sun had set by the time the *Explorer* rounded the north end of Copper Key. Located nine miles west of Key West, the thirty-acre island had a beautiful sandy beach with towering palm trees on the south side. Isaiah Wright had built himself a huge mansion close to the shore, complete with a guest house nearby. This part of the island was idyllic. But the north side was lined with a rising rocky shore leading up to a jagged cliff face. Reefs close to the shore made landing a boat here impossible. Approaching without being seen by Wright's patrolling boats also posed a problem.

Anthony cut the *Explorer*'s engine and walked to the stern of the boat.

"Can you see anything?" he asked.

Noah was training a pair of binoculars on the shoreline. "The moon's helping, but it's still hard to make out much. I remember Dad saying there's an opening to the cave above the waterline, and one below."

"We should swim in the underwater entrance so no one sees us," Anthony said.

"Can we shine some light on the shore?" Noah asked.

"Just for a second." Anthony trained a large spotlight on the shore. "We don't want to attract attention." He flicked a switch and a bright beam of light hit the shoreline.

"Wait. There it is." Noah handed the binoculars to Anthony, then adjusted the spotlight. "Right by that outcropping of rocks."

Anthony peered through the binoculars. "I wonder how deep the water is there."

"And if there are barracudas," Juan Carlo chimed in. He'd changed clothes and looked much more comfortable in shorts and a tee shirt.

"I wish we could get a bit closer," Anthony said. "Better turn off the light."

"Will you dive now?" Juan Carlo asked.

Noah shook his head. "We'd have to use underwater lights. If patrolling boats came by, the lights would alert them."

"We can come back in the morning and dive once the sun is up. We'll moor the boat out far enough where Wright can't tell us where to be. I'll dive over there while you two stay with the boat. I'll explore the cave and see what I can find. If anything goes wrong, you hightail it out of here and get Chief Burton."

"Uh-oh. It looks like we have more than barracudas to deal with." Noah had the binoculars again. He reached over and turned on the spotlight.

"What do you mean?" Anthony asked.

"Watch over by the cave entrance." The dark water shimmered in the spotlight, and periodically a fin broke through the surface, cutting through the water like a silver knife.

"Sharks," Anthony said.

"That's bad," Juan Carlo shuddered.

"They must be feeding on something in the cave," Noah said.

Anthony nodded. "Just what we need."

"How do you get in there if the sharks are there?" Juan Carlo asked.

"Go in the opening above the waterline," Anthony shrugged.

"It's up on the left."

Anthony took the binoculars and studied the cave. "You're right. But, man, that's a small hole. I don't know if I can squeeze through that." He cut the spotlight power again.

"Then I'll go," Noah said, his jaw locked in determination.

"It's too dangerous," Juan Carlo said.

"We'll both go," Anthony said.

"We can swim over to the left," Noah pointed

south of the entrance. "Then we'll get out of the water at those rocks. We'll leave the tanks there and climb over to the entrance."

"You sound pretty sure of yourself," Anthony said.

"I've played around in places like that before," Noah said.

Anthony scrutinized the shoreline again. "I don't see any other way." He gave the binoculars to Juan Carlo. "We'll come back tomorrow. If we start at first light, we can be back at the house in plenty of time for the phone call."

"This is too dangerous," Juan Carlo repeated. "There must be another way."

"Not in the time we have," Noah said. "We have to find those glass pieces before noon tomorrow."

In the distance, the revving sound of a motorboat pierced the darkness.

"Wright's patrol," Anthony said. "They saw the spotlight. Let's get out of here!"

He sped to the cabin and started the engine. The *Explorer* churned through the inky water, leaving Copper Key behind.

CHAPTER SEVEN

SHARKS

Friday dawned warm, with gentle breezes stirring the palm trees on the south side of Copper Key. Off the north shore, the *Explorer* sat anchored in the thirty-foot depths.

"Here's the radio." Noah showed Juan Carlo a VHF marine radio. "It's set to the Coast Guard channel. You hit this button and then start talking into the receiver."

"I understand," Juan Carlo said.

"You tell them the name of the boat, '*Explorer*', three times," Noah continued. "Give them your location. I've written it down for you." He handed Juan Carlo a piece of paper. "Then tell them what's going on."

"If we don't come back by noon, or if Isaiah Wright's boats come after you, go for help. Use the radio, or here's my cell phone," Anthony handed it to Juan Carlo. "You won't get reception out here, but once closer to Key West, you can speed dial 21. That's Chief Burton's number."

Juan Carlo threw him a puzzled look. "Speed

dial?"

"Just press 21 and hit the call button," Anthony showed him. "If he doesn't answer, dial 911."

"Sí," Juan Carlo said.

They went aft, where the diving gear was laid out. Noah and Anthony donned the gear in silence.

"Be careful," Juan Carlo said. He held a fishing rod and would pretend to fish while Noah and Anthony were exploring the cave.

Noah adjusted his mask, bit down on the regulator, and signaled he was ready to go.

"If we see any sharks, you go where I go," Anthony instructed Noah.

Noah hopped off the boat platform and into the water. Anthony jumped in and swam up beside him. Noah gave Anthony a thumbs-up, then started kicking. He shot through the water. The only sound was his breathing through the regulator.

Ten minutes after leaving the *Explorer*, they approached the shore. Noah kicked hard against a strong current. It buffeted him toward a reef and Noah stuck out his hand to keep from slamming against it. He swam hard, and he and Anthony soon found a place where they could climb out of the water.

They had brought flashlights with them, so Noah set his on a rock, then tugged the fins off his feet. He set them on the rock with the flashlight, then pushed his mask up on his forehead. He found an underwater toehold for his feet, pushed up with his legs, and grabbed the rocks. He then hefted himself out of the water, pulling himself forward until he could get up on his knees. He worked out of the tanks, setting them and his fins in a crack behind a large rock.

Behind him, Anthony struggled to get out. His upper body was halfway out of the water when he slipped. Splash!

"How did you get up there so easily?" he muttered.

"Use your toes to grip the rock," Noah said. "Like a monkey would."

"Like a monkey," Anthony growled. "I still can't find a foothold." Noah reached over to give him a hand, and Anthony managed to lift himself out of the water.

Anthony hid his dive gear with Noah's and they checked out their surroundings. Some of the rocks were smooth from the pounding waves spraying them, but others were rough and jagged. Farther down, they could see the cave opening near the cliff face. The opening was not much bigger around than a car tire.

"I'm not sure if I can fit through that," Anthony said.

Noah didn't reply. One of them had to get in the cave and find the hidden box, if it was there. He stepped forward. "Ouch! The rocks hurt my feet."

"Careful," Anthony chided him. They worked their way across the rocks, treading lightly. After what seemed like years, but was only minutes, they arrived at the cave. Noah bent down and looked inside.

"I can't see a thing."

He was about to shine the flashlight into the cave when Anthony yanked his arm.

"A boat's coming!" Anthony hissed. He jerked his head around, looking for a place to hide. "Behind that rock!"

Noah scooted after Anthony. They scrunched down and waited. A powerboat zoomed by, its high-pitched engine loudly announcing its presence. The noise faded, then came back.

Anthony leaned over Noah, putting his mouth right by Noah's ear. "They're taking a second pass," he murmured. "Stay down."

Noah held his breath as the sound of the engine died.

"They're probably checking the shoreline with binoculars," Anthony whispered. "Don't move."

They stayed huddled so long that Noah's muscles ached. Finally, they heard the boat's engine rev up and the boat continued down the shore.

"Let's go," Anthony said.

They hurried back to the cave entrance. Noah had to lie down and belly crawl through the opening. He couldn't see beyond a few feet. He flicked on his flashlight. The beam bounded off black wet walls. He stood only a foot above the water. The cave was large, with a ceiling about eight feet above his head. Noah stood on a thin ledge that ran around a third of the walls, stopping where there was a small crevice. The crevice ran from the ceiling right down the cave wall, disappearing into the water.

"Hold on, I'm stuck."

Noah turned around. Anthony was halfway through but his hips were stuck in the hole. He pushed with his elbows, freeing himself.

"That was tight." Anthony rubbed at a cut on his chest. It wasn't deep, but blood oozed from it.

Anthony shone his light around the cave, then on the water. Two sharks zipped around, then darted out of the cave.

"I'll bet the chest is over somewhere in that crevice," Noah said.

"That's a good bet. Think you can make it over there?" Anthony asked.

Noah nodded. He worked along the wall, his bare feet gripping tiny footholds in the wet rocks. At one point the ledge was no wider than a baseball bat. Noah reached out and grabbed a rock jutting out from the cave wall. He placed his toes down on the ledge and leaned forward. His foot slipped and he dangled for a moment, his hands clutching the rock outcropping.

"Noah!" Anthony yelled. His voice echoed loudly in the cave.

Noah's foot kicked the water. A second later, a shark snapped the water where his foot had been.

Noah regained his balance and pushed himself onward. "I'm okay," he said. He had to take a deep breath to calm himself. His hands shook. Below, the sharks flitted back and forth, attracted by the movement.

"Can you get to the crevice?"

"Yes," Noah said. The last few feet were easier and then Noah was perched on a small rock shelf.

"Good job," Anthony said as he joined Noah.

Noah shined his light up into the crevice. "I don't see anything up there."

Anthony trained his light up the cleft as well, and peered over Noah's shoulder. "It narrows up there." He stepped back and looked down into the water. "Maybe the box is stuck down there."

They aimed their flashlights on the water.

"I can't see very far," Noah said.

"Me, either."

"We'll have to check it out."

Anthony nodded. He touched his chest, where the cut still trickled blood. "This will attract the sharks."

"Then I go." Noah swallowed the lump in his throat. They both watched a shark that swam around below them. "We have to keep them away from me."

"I'll go over by the entrance," Anthony said. "And I'll try and distract them. See if you can slide down the crevice, that way you'll stay out of reach."

Noah stared down at the water, trying to quell his fear. "Sharks don't normally harm humans," he said, more to himself than Anthony. "They attack when they mistake a human for food."

"Just go slowly," Anthony said as he made his way back over the ledge to the cave entrance. "Okay," he said when he arrived. He hit the water with his hand, jerking his hand back up quickly. A shark darted over near him, its fin slicing through the water.

"I wish I had my diving gear and spear gun," Noah said.

"It wouldn't have fit through this entrance." Anthony hit the water again.

Noah sat down on the rock ledge, letting his feet slide into the water in the crevice. The shark stayed over by Anthony. Noah grabbed a rock with one hand, holding the flashlight with the other. He felt his arm strain as he lowered himself into the water. He took a deep breath right before his head went under the surface. He barely fit into the crack. Noah knew he could hold his breath for more than a minute, but that still was precious little time. He shone the light around. Nothing but rock.

Noah pushed down into the crevice, but it quickly tapered off. He would have to go into the cave itself. Fighting to calm himself, Noah edged out of the crevice. The shark darted nearby. Noah plastered himself against the wall of the cave and froze. From above, Anthony smacked the water and the shark turned and swam away.

Noah twisted around and swam down, the light

beam illuminating the crevice as it thinned and then disappeared. He didn't see anything resembling a metal box. He scrutinized the cave floor. No box. He felt movement and swiveled back around. Another shark was in the cave, coming toward him. Noah let himself float upward, hugging the rock wall. The shark swam closer. Noah wanted to scream, but it would do no good. He was out of air and needed to get to the surface. Just then, the other shark rocketed up in front of the first shark. They tangled for a second. Noah's head burst into the air. He simultaneously sucked in great gasps of air and pushed himself into the crevice. The sharks swam by, too big to get into the crack where Noah was.

"Come on, get out." Anthony was hurrying toward him. "I saw that other shark and tried to distract him, but it wasn't working anymore."

Noah tossed his flashlight on the ledge and hauled himself out of the water. He sat for a moment, dripping as he caught his breath.

"I didn't see anything," he huffed. "The crack gets narrower. If Alfonso stuck a chest there, it's gone."

Noah stood up as Anthony joined him. "If it's somewhere else below, we have to get rid of the sharks before we search."

"Where else could it be?" Anthony mused. They scanned the cave, but saw no other hiding place for a chest.

"Maybe we have the wrong place," Noah said

dejectedly. But what did that mean for his parents?

Anthony let out a big sigh. "We better get back to the *Explorer*. We'll just have to tell your parents' captors that we need more time."

They started back across the ledge. Anthony gripped with his toes much better now, but halfway toward the entrance, he slipped in the same place that Noah did.

"Whoa!" He thrashed out with one hand, snatching at the rock wall above his head. But instead of giving him a handhold, a huge chunk of rock broke away. "What the…" Anthony let go of the rock. It splashed into the water. The sharks darted over, stirring the water. Noah clutched Anthony's other hand, pulling him back. Anthony gripped another part of the wall, his knuckles white.

"That was too close," he finally managed to say.

Noah glanced up where the rock had been. "Hey, look at that."

A gaping hole yawned at them.

"You don't…" Noah's voice trailed away.

"Uh-huh." Anthony grinned excitedly. He reached up and felt into the hole. "I can feel something metal."

"That's it!" Noah said.

Anthony set his flashlight down and searched for footholds. He climbed up the rock wall until his head was even with the hole. "Shine your light up here."

Noah complied. "What do you see?"

"It's a box! Just like Juan Carlo described. It's not very big. I think I can get it." He grunted and groaned, reached in with one hand and dragged out a small metal box.

"Here, take it." Anthony lowered the box. "Hurry, my legs and arms are hurting."

Noah grabbed the box, almost losing his balance in the process. He put the box between himself and the cave wall, pressing against it.

"Okay, hand it to me," Anthony said when he returned to the ledge.

Noah put a hand underneath the box and eased it over to Anthony.

"Got it." They made their way back to the cave entrance, where the ledge was wider.

"Is it in there?" Noah asked eagerly.

"There's a padlock on it." Anthony pulled at it. "I can't get it. Let's take it outside and find a rock, and I'll try to break the lock off."

Anthony crawled out of the entrance. Noah pushed the box out, then crept out himself, blinking in the harsh sunlight.

"Quick!" Anthony waved at him. "There's another patrol boat."

They ran and hid until the boat passed by.

"Let's open this before another one comes by," Anthony said.

"Here's a good rock." Noah handed a softball-sized rock to Anthony.

Anthony seized the rock and slammed it against the lock. He hit it again and the lock snapped. Anthony pulled away the broken pieces and gently opened the lid.

Inside were moldy papers, a stack of old money, and a small leather pouch that was weathered and cracked.

Anthony stared at Noah with eyes wide. Anthony picked up the pouch. Leather pieces flaked away as he opened it. Inside they saw two round pieces of glass. They had etchings on them, and one had a tiny shaft of metal sticking from its center.

"We found it," Noah breathed slowly, relieved.

Anthony nodded in satisfaction. He took out one of the glass pieces, holding it by its edges. Lines ran across its surfaces, and they could see tiny lettering. "Fascinating," he murmured.

Reality set in as they heard a boat again.

"A boat shouldn't be patrolling again so soon," Anthony said. He hurriedly put the glass piece back in the leather pouch. He placed the pouch in a pocket of his swim trunks. "They must be getting suspicious. We'll leave the box here. I don't want to carry it back through the water and ruin anything else in it. If Juan Carlo wants it, he can come back for it later."

"Let's go," Noah said. "We have to get back before the kidnappers call again."

They both knew Noah was right. They were

running out of time.

They rushed back to the cache where they had hidden their diving gear.

"Watch for those sharks," Anthony said as they dressed. He stooped down and splashed water on his chest, washing off the blood.

"This isn't good," he scowled. "A shark can smell blood from miles away."

"At least it's not bleeding anymore," Noah said.

Anthony forced a small smile. "Just watch my back."

They stepped into the water and swam back to the *Explorer*.

CHAPTER EIGHT

THE SCUBACRAFT

"This is amazing!" Juan Carlo said. "Just think. This has been in my family for almost two hundred years."

Noah and Anthony had swum back to the *Explorer* without incident. Juan Carlo had said that a patrol boat had gone by. He had waved at the boat as he fished, and after watching the *Explorer* for a few minutes, the boat sped away. Anthony and Noah were now showing Juan Carlo the etched-glass pieces.

"Where is the spyglass?" Juan Carlo asked. They had brought the spyglass tubing with them, storing it in the safe. Noah fetched it. He took the spyglass out of the box and handed it to Juan Carlo.

"This must be how it works." Noah watched in fascination as Juan Carlo carefully twisted the end of spyglass, loosening it. Then he popped the lens out. Juan Carlo switched it with the etched-glass piece with the metal rod in it. He attached the two etched pieces of glass to the rod.

"Ingenious," Anthony said in awe. He was piloting

the boat as he talked, but he had a hard time keeping his eyes on the water ahead of him.

"We can shine light through it at home and project the map onto a wall," Noah said. "But how will we know how to rotate the glass pieces?"

"We'll just have to play around with it," Anthony said. "We'll be at the harbor soon, so you won't have to wait long."

***

Back at the house, they fixed lunch and ate quickly.

"I've got a diving light," Noah said as he chomped on a tuna sandwich. "Let's turn out the lights in the living room and shut the blinds. We can shine the light through the spyglass and project it onto the wall next to the bookshelves."

In a few minutes, they were ready. Anthony turned off the lights.

"Here we go." Juan Carlo held the spyglass up while Anthony shined the powerful diving light through one end of it. An image with lines and curves appeared on the wall, like a pencil drawing.

"Wow," Noah said. "It works."

"But it doesn't make sense," Juan Carlo said. He twisted one glass piece for a moment. "Does this image mean anything to you two?"

Noah and Anthony shook their heads. Juan Carlo fiddled with the spyglass some more, but it didn't help.

"Juan Carlo, you said that there's supposed to be lines on the map that will tell us where to look. 'X' marks the spot, remember?" Noah asked.

"Maybe we don't have it projected on the wall correctly," Juan Carlo mused.

"Let me try," Anthony said. He turned the pieces slowly. "Hey, there are notches on the edges of the two glass pieces. I didn't notice that." He lined up the notches and studied the wall. "I have no idea what that is."

"It's some islands, but it doesn't look like Key West." Noah taped pieces of computer paper to the wall. "I'll trace it."

He took a pen and drew lines on the paper. As he worked, he knew he was tracing a map of some of the Florida Keys. But since there were so many islands in the Keys, he couldn't tell which ones he had drawn. He also traced some Spanish writing on the map.

"How could someone write that small on the glass pieces?" Noah asked.

"He must've used a magnifying glass to help him," Anthony suggested.

"Extraordinary," Juan Carlo said.

Noah finished tracing the map and they put the spyglass back in the box. Noah glanced at the clock on the wall. It was almost time for the phone call from his parents' captors.

"I still don't see any lines that would mark a

specific place on the map," Anthony said.

"We must still be missing a piece that attaches to the etched-glass pieces," Noah sighed.

Juan Carlo nodded. "Alfonso must have kept it with the spyglass."

"Then it's still somewhere around the wreck," Noah said. "But we don't have time to find it now."

"Let's talk to Chief Burton about what to do," Juan Carlo said.

"What else can we figure out before the police get here?" Anthony fingered the writing on the map. "That's Spanish, isn't it?"

"Yes," Juan Carlo nodded. He stood up and went to the wall. "This means –"

The chime of the doorbell interrupted him. Noah raced to the door.

Chief Burton stood on the porch with Detective Shaw.

"Come on in," Noah said. They followed him into the kitchen.

"Have you heard anything?' Chief Burton asked. "Anybody following you?"

"Not that I know of," Noah answered.

Juan Carlo introduced himself to Chief Burton. Chief Burton and Detective Shaw sat down at the table.

"We're still missing one part of the spyglass," Noah said.

Chief Burton grimaced. "Okay," he said after a

moment. "Tell them that. It could buy us more time. By the way, we found the Honda. It was abandoned on a street on Stork Island."

"Did you find any clues as to what happened?" Juan Carlo asked.

Detective Shaw spoke up. "Nothing. No sign of foul play. And no clues either. The car was wiped clean."

"What about the kidnappers?" Noah asked. "I still have to talk to them."

"Here's what we're doing," Chief Burton said. "We've got taps on the phone line. When the kidnappers call, try and keep them on the line as long as you can."

"What do I say?" Noah asked.

"Ask for more time. Tell them you haven't found the spyglass yet. Ask how your parents are. Tell them you want to know if your parents are hurt in any way."

"Okay," Noah said.

Just then the phone rang. Noah picked it up and hit the speaker button.

"Hello?"

"We will do the exchange tonight," a low voice said. Everyone in the room held their breath.

"But I don't have the entire map," Noah said.

"You do, and you will bring it to us."

"I want to know if my parents are okay," Noah raised his voice.

The caller ignored him. "You and Anthony take

the *Explorer* out to the Marquesas Keys at midnight tonight. Anchor a mile off the east coast. Noah, you will swim due east from the boat. Bring the map with you. A boat will pick you up. Once we know that you have brought what we want, we will tell you where to pick up your parents."

"But I can't swim and carry the map as well," Noah said.

"Don't deviate from the instructions in any way. No police. We will be watching. If you want to see your parents again, do as we say."

Brrr! The sound of the dial tone filled the kitchen. Noah stared at the phone, his jaw hanging open.

"He's smart," Detective Shaw said. "He knew to keep the conversation short. That's why he didn't answer any of your questions."

Chief Burton's cell phone chirped. "Yeah?" He nodded a couple of times. "I'll be in shortly." He hung up and turned to them. "No luck on tracing the call. He didn't stay on long enough."

Noah frowned.

"It's okay, son," Chief Burton said. "You did the best you could." He stood up. "Anthony, how long will it take to go out to the Marquesas Keys in the *Explorer*?"

"About half an hour."

Detective Shaw rubbed his jaw, thinking. "Here's what we'll do. I'm sure they'll be watching, so we can't have a patrol boat anywhere around. But we can keep in touch with the *Explorer* by radio." He turned to Chief Burton. "We'll get a stand-in for Noah, someone to take his place. That person will swim out instead of Noah."

"I have to go," Noah said. "Didn't you hear them? If anything goes wrong, what'll they do to my parents? I can't let anything bad happen to them."

"They could be bluffing," Detective Shaw said.

"It's a chance we'll have to take." Chief Burton bit his lip. "Shaw, find me a stand-in. Officer Perez is small and thin. We could use him." He put a hand on Noah's shoulder. "Don't worry. We'll put a waterproof transmitter in a pair of swim trunks so we can keep track of the stand-in. We're going to get everything set up and I'll come by here later today." He turned to Anthony. "You can pilot the *Explorer*. You and the officer will drive from here, just in case anyone's watching."

"Okay," Anthony said.

"You do exactly like they said. We'll have the officer deliver the spyglass. Once they have that, they should release your parents."

"Are you sure?" Noah asked, worry in his voice.

"Yes," Chief Burton smiled at him hopefully. "They want the map, not your parents."

Noah forced a smile in return, but he was scared that things would go wrong.

***

"That's not going to work," Anthony said after Chief Burton left. "A stand-in isn't going to fool the kidnappers."

Noah lip trembled. "I don't want anything to happen to my parents. I don't care what Chief Burton said, I have to deliver the map."

"It is too dangerous for you," Juan Carlo said.

"No, it's not," Noah said. He turned to Anthony. "We can take the *Explorer* out there. Dad has some transmitters that we can put in my swim trunks, so you can track me. I'll deliver the spyglass and they'll let Mom and Dad go. Then we'll call Chief Burton and let them know what happened."

"I don't know," Anthony hesitated.

"Come on!" Noah said. "You know we can do this. You take me out there, I'll give them the map, and then you can call Chief Burton. It's the only way!"

"I don't know." Anthony rubbed his jaw. "Juan Carlo's right. It's too dangerous. If something happened to you, I could never face your parents."

"I can do this," Noah pleaded. "If the police are spotted, who knows what'll happen. We have to do this ourselves."

Anthony nodded slowly. "Okay, let's do it."

"But –" Juan Carlo said.

"Noah's right. Trying to use a stand-in won't fool the kidnappers," Anthony interrupted him. "This is the only way to get Noah's parents back safely."

Juan Carlo muttered in Spanish. "Sí. But if anything happens to you or Noah, I don't think I can forgive myself."

"We'll be fine," Anthony said.

Noah thought about those words later, when things did go awry.

***

At ten o'clock, Noah and Anthony drove to the marina. Chief Burton had called that afternoon and said that Officer Perez, the stand-in for Noah, would come by at eleven and go with Anthony to the marina. By leaving earlier, Noah and Anthony avoided Chief Burton, who would surely put a stop to their plans.

Phil Harris was not happy about having someone interrupt his night watch. But Chief Burton had obviously cleared things, because Phil gave them little trouble, other than a snide comment about them showing up earlier than he expected.

Anthony and Noah untied the *Explorer* in silence. Anthony turned on the boat's lights and guided it past other vessels out into the open water. Noah stared at the dark water as they cruised toward the Marquesas Keys.

After a while, Anthony cut the engine. "We'll wait here."

"What do you think Chief Burton will do when he finds out we left earlier?" Noah asked.

"He's going to be angry," Anthony shuddered. "But I doubt Chief Burton will send a police cruiser out here because he'll know that'll put you and your parents at risk. He's going to have to sit tight until he hears from us."

Noah paced nervously, pausing every few moments to gaze out into the darkness.

Anthony said nothing, but kept looking at his watch. "It's midnight," he finally announced.

"I'll be seeing my parents soon," Noah said, trying to think positively. They went aft, where Noah could dive into the water.

"Make sure the transmitter is on," Anthony said. He had showed Noah how to work it earlier in the day.

Noah felt in a tiny pocket inside his new swim trunks. "It's on." He slipped into the water. He couldn't see more than a couple feet below him.

"Kind of spooky," he said. The moon flitted in and out of silvery clouds.

"It's okay. Good luck," Anthony said. "Just swim out that way. I'll be watching with the binoculars."

"Okay." Noah struck out, using a front crawl stroke. He was a strong swimmer, but he had difficulty in the choppy waters. Carrying the box made swimming harder, too. He swam until his arms and shoulders ached. Noah paused and treaded water with one arm. He glanced behind him. He was a hundred yards from the *Explorer*. Noah couldn't see anything around him. His breathing raced, both from exertion and fear. He swam farther and stopped. What if this was just a wild goose chase? He could end up drowning before anyone rescued him.

Then he heard a speedboat nearing. A spotlight swept the water, coming to rest on him. He squinted at the bright light. It suddenly went off and he blinked, his eyes adjusting to the abrupt darkness. The boat engine died. Noah jerked as its hull suddenly came by him. Powerful hands snatched him under the shoulders and roughly hauled him into the boat.

"Stay down," a menacing voice ordered him. He felt a gun poke into his back.

Noah huddled in the bottom of the boat, shaking. He turned his head cautiously. Three men stood over him. One was short and stocky, with a shaved head. He wore a swimsuit and no shirt. His chest was as wide as a barrel. The second man was taller, with a flat face and crooked nose. Noah tipped his head to the side. The third man, holding the gun to his back, had spiked blond hair – Dave 'The Wrench' Dixon. He and the man with the flat face had diving gear on.

"Let me see it." The man with the flat face nudged Noah with his foot. Noah handed him the box with the spyglass in it.

"This is the map?" Noah didn't say anything. Dave hit him on the back of the head. "Is this it?"

"Yes," Noah said. His scalp hurt where Dave had struck him.

"Good. Scheff can make the Winters figure it out."

They didn't intend to release his parents! Noah coughed, his mind in a whirl. *What do I do now?* he thought.

"That assistant kid's bringing the *Explorer* this way," the man with the flat face said.

"Stand up." Dave yanked Noah's hair.

Noah struggled to his feet, swaying with the motion of the boat. "Put these on." The man with the flat face held a pair of swim trunks. "Just in case you tried to pull something, like putting a transmitter in your trunks."

Noah felt his heart cave in. His captors were taking no chances. He changed into the trunks, almost losing his balance. He set his swim trunks in the bottom of the boat. There was no way to transfer the transmitter into his new trunks.

"Now this," the bald man said. He helped Noah into a diving tank. Once it was on, he stuck the regulator in Noah's mouth.

"Gimme your hands," the man with the flat face growled at Noah.

Noah put his hands in front of him. The man with the flat face locked a pair of handcuffs on him.

"Turn around."

Noah did as he was told.

The bald man wrapped rope around Noah's arms and legs, trussing him up like a mummy. He held Noah as the others put on their masks.

"There's the Scubacraft," Dave said. He gestured over the side of the boat.

Noah looked where Dave was pointing. Below the water's surface, Noah saw the dull glow of an underwater Scubacraft. He had heard about this new type of craft. It was powered by twin engines and could scoot over the water at fifty miles-per-hour. And it could also run underwater. The Scubacraft cost over a hundred thousand dollars.

"You take the boat back toward Marquesas," Dave said to the bald man. "Pete will be there. Scuttle the boat."

Where are we going? Noah thought.

Dave set his gun down and snatched up a large wrench. He stuck it in the waistband of his diving suit.

"You give me any problems, you'll get a smack with this," he snarled. He turned on Noah's air and checked the regulator. "Start breathing."

Noah sucked in a breath. The next second, Dave picked him up and threw him overboard. Noah struck the water with a resounding splatter. He fought panic as he sank down. He could breath, but with his hands and legs tied, he was as helpless. He twisted around, seeing the Scubacraft's light. A man was driving it, but Noah could barely see him. Then hands grabbed him.

Dave and the man with the flat face pulled him along as they swam to the Scubacraft. They tied Noah to the Scubacraft and hung on to the rails. The Scubacraft whirred through the water, away from the boat, even farther away from the *Explorer*. Noah didn't have a mask on, and the rushing water hurt his eyes. He closed them, feeling completely blind and powerless.

Anthony will think I'm still in the boat, Noah thought. *He couldn't have seen them throw me over the side.*

He counted in order to keep himself calm. His body jiggled back and forth as the Scubacraft gained speed. Noah kept counting. After reaching a hundred, he started over. Minutes passed by, and the Scubacraft finally slowed to a stop. Noah opened his eyes. He saw the white underside of what looked like a large luxury yacht.

"How far had they gone from the *Explorer*?" Noah wondered. He prayed that Anthony had contacted Chief Burton and they were searching for him now.

Dave and the man with the flat face untied him. The Scubacraft drove off, disappearing in the darkness. Dave pulled Noah to the surface. The man with the flat face emerged beside them.

"Untie him," Dave said, holding Noah up.

The man with the flat face slit the ropes and Noah kicked with his feet to stay afloat.

"Climb up the ladder." Noah saw an aluminum ladder to climb aboard the yacht. He reached for a rung, then swung his handcuffed hands at Dave, striking him on the cheek. Noah sank below the surface. Dave yanked him by the hair.

"Let me go!" Noah sputtered at him.

Dave pulled out the wrench and swiped it across Noah's face. "You pull a stunt like that again, I'll do more than hit you. Now get up that ladder." He shoved Noah hard at the ladder.

Noah crashed against the ladder, his breath knocked away. He could feel a bump growing on his cheek where Dave hit him. He gasped as he awkwardly climbed up. A man with a Glock semi-automatic pistol stood waiting on deck. He dragged Noah up the last couple of feet. Noah stood in his swim trunks, dripping wet. Dave and the man with the flat face came on board.

"Any problems?" the man with the Glock asked.

"Everything's fine," Dave answered. "Take him below."

The man with the Glock prodded Noah with it, indicating he should walk ahead of him. Noah's eyes darted around, trying to memorize his surroundings. They walked along a narrow corridor with windows to rooms, but Noah couldn't see inside them. They came to stairs and went down.

"In here." The man with the Glock opened a door and stepped aside. Noah entered a large stateroom. It had a big bed, folding doors which he assumed opened to a closet, and a small bathroom.

"Lie down on the bed."

Noah's mouth went dry. What were they going to do? He got on the bed and lay down on his back. Dave and the man with the flat face entered the room. Dave had something in his hand.

"Hold him," Dave told the others.

The man with the flat face and the man with the Glock grabbed Noah. Noah twisted and kicked, but the men were too strong. Dave stood beside him. Now Noah saw what he held: a syringe.

"Nighty-night," Dave said in a sing-song voice. He bent down and twisted Noah's arm. He found a vein in the arm and plunged the needle in.

"Let me go," Noah struggled.

The room suddenly spun. Dizziness passed over him. Then darkness.

CHAPTER NINE

CHANG AND A KNIFE

Noah awoke with a start. He was lying on a king-sized four-poster bed in another large room. Hazy light filtered in through the blinds of a large bay window. Noah blinked a couple of times and moaned. He felt groggy, and his headed pounded from a headache. He raised his arms to rub his eyes, but they jerked to a stop after about a foot. He looked over at one hand. It was tied with rope to the bedpost. He glanced at his other arm. It was tied as well. His feet were also lashed with rope to the posts at the end of the bed.

He flopped his head back on the pillow. "Ouch," Noah muttered as his head throbbed. He lay quietly for a few minutes until the thudding stopped. Then he assessed his situation. He couldn't hear the yacht's engine, or the motion of the sea. Conclusion: he was no longer on a boat. But if he was on land, where was he?

Someone had dressed him as well. He had on khaki shorts, a blue tee shirt, and tennis shoes. He pulled at the ropes, but could not free his hands. As he worked to untie his hands, he noticed that the handcuffs had left bruises on his wrists.

Noah studied the room more closely. Across from him, an expensive painting hung on the wall. The furniture looked expensive, too. Someone with money had furnished this room. But who?

The answer strolled through the door a half hour later.

"Ah, I see you're awake." A man turned on the overhead light. Noah squinted at two men who entered the room.

An Asian man with broad shoulders and thick arms guarded the door. He held a Smith & Wesson pistol, and a knife in a leather holster hung on his belt. Sweat glistened from his bald head.

The other man stood at the end of the bed. He was dressed in white shorts and a silk shirt. He was tall, well over six feet, and thin and pale as a piece of white paper. He had unusually long fingers, Noah noticed, and shoulder-length gray hair pulled into a ponytail. Noah had seen his picture before, in the society section of the Key West Citizen, the local paper.

"You're Isaiah Wright!"

"I see you know me." Wright tapped his long fingers together as he talked. His voice was high-pitched and reedy.

"Why am I here?" Noah asked. "I gave you the spyglass. You have what you want."

"Not entirely." Tap, tap, went Wright's fingers. "I

still need to know how to interpret the map. That's where you come in."

"I won't help you," Noah spat.

"Ah, but you will," Wright smiled slightly. "I assure you, you will."

"Is the emerald worth this?" Noah asked. "You'll be charged with kidnapping. You'll go to jail."

"Ha, ha." Wright leaned forward, laughing. "My dear boy, your courage is admirable, however misguided." His eyes narrowed. "You're out of your league. I suggest you cooperate, and I will let you go unharmed."

"What about my parents?"

"We'll get to that." Wright turned to the Asian man. "Chang, untie him."

Chang marched to the bed and used the knife to slice effortlessly through the ropes. He gestured with the knife and Noah swung his legs over the side of the bed and stood up. His legs tingled with numbness and Noah put a hand back on the bed to steady himself. Then Chang grabbed him by the shoulder and pinched him hard.

"Ow!" Noah yelped.

"Chang can do much more than that," Wright said. "Don't give him any trouble."

They marched out of the room and down a long hallway.

"You asked me if the emerald was worth all this,"

Wright said, pausing in front of a heavy wooden door. "If you'll indulge me for a moment."

Wright opened the door and showed Noah into a room filled with glass cases and paintings on the walls.

"The items in this room are priceless," he said, waving a hand around. "It's a collection of art and jewels worthy of a king."

Noah couldn't help gawking. Each case displayed countless amazing items: swords and shields, necklaces and rings, all sparkled in the soft light. Huge rare-cut gems sat on velvet pillows. Noah saw diamonds, rubies, and other precious stones.

Wright pointed at a sword.

"This once belonged to the Crown Prince of Austria." Wright gazed lovingly at the sword. "Isn't it spectacular?"

"That was stolen from a museum in Austria a year ago," Noah said.

"Stolen!" Wright sniffed. "Such a vulgar word. I merely appropriated it for better use."

"What do you mean?"

"Can you imagine all those people visiting the museum and passing by this priceless treasure as if it's nothing? Such a fine piece doesn't impress them at all." Wright shook his head in disgust. "I brought it here and now display it for my friends. Only a rare few like us can truly appreciate the beauty that is collected in this room."

Noah stared at Wright. Only a madman would harm people to get what he wanted. Isaiah Wright belonged in prison, not on his own privately owned island.

"You're crazy," Noah said.

Wright tapped his fingers together. "Someday you'll understand what I mean." He flicked a finger at Noah. "Come now."

They exited the room and turned right. They walked to the end of the hall, coming to a stairway. They climbed up, Noah between Wright and Chang. At the top were four doorways. Wright went to the third, opened it, and gestured for Noah to go in.

Noah stepped into the room. It was empty except for a small wooden table and one wooden chair. A small television and a video camera sat at one end of the table. The walls were padded with heavy tarps.

"The room is soundproofed," Wright said. "You can scream all you want, but no one will hear you."

Chang guided Noah to the chair and thrust him down. Noah grimaced. Chang extracted some cord from his pocket. He tied Noah's legs to separate chair legs, then tied his arms to each side of the chair back.

"Excellent," Wright said. "Now it's time for you to help me."

"Forget it," Noah said.

Wright laughed. He strode to the end of the table and tapped a button on the television. The monitor blinked on. Noah gasped at what he saw. His mother and father were sitting in two chairs, tied up just like he was. Both had gags in their mouths.

"Mom! Dad!" Noah shouted.

"They can't hear you at the moment," Wright said. He picked up the camera and pointed it at his face. He pushed a switch. "Paul, can you hear me?"

"Yes, boss," a deep voice cackled from a speaker in the television.

"Good. And Frank and Riley can hear me?"

Noah looked at the television. Frank and Riley both nodded their heads.

"Paul, they can see their monitor?"

"We're all set up," Paul answered.

"Excellent. Take their gags off."

Noah watched as a huge hulk of a man came into the picture. He went behind Noah's parents and removed their gags.

"We've told you everything we know," Frank sputtered. "Please, just let my wife go."

"I wish I could do that," Wright said as he held the camera at arms' length, pointed to his own face. "And I think you can be of further assistance."

"But we've told you…" Riley began.

"I think not, Mrs. Winter," Wright interrupted her. "I have someone who will help persuade you to work with me." Wright turned the camera on Noah.

"Noah!" Riley cried out.

"Noah, son! Don't you harm him," Frank yelled. He twisted in his chair, straining against the ropes.

Wright nodded at Chang. Chang bent down and untied Noah's right arm. He yanked the arm up, slammed Noah's hand on the table, and spread the fingers apart. Then he unsheathed his knife. Noah trembled. Chang placed the knife over Noah's pinky, just touching the skin.

"What did you say about harming him?" Wright said.

"No!" Riley and Frank both shouted.

"It would be a shame to lose a finger, and at such a young age," Wright said.

Noah shook, fighting back tears.

"We'll do whatever you want, just don't hurt him!" Riley pleaded.

"Please," Frank said. His voice quivered.

Wright stared at Noah for a second, then jerked his head. Chang backed away. Wright turned the camera back on himself.

"Very well," he said at last. "I will be there shortly. And we will interpret the map correctly." He inhaled, then let his breath out slowly. "It's such a shame to have to resort to threats like this."

Noah let his hand fall off the table, back at his side. He nerves prickled with a growing anger. Now that the imminent threat was over, he fumed about what Wright might do to his parents.

Wright turned off the television. He set the camera on the table.

"Come, Chang." Wright strode to the door. "I'll need your help. I'm sure the Winters will be somewhat distraught after this ghastly episode." At the door, he turned around. "Someone will be here shortly to take you back to your room. If you want to keep all your fingers, I suggest you mind your manners."

Noah gulped as the door slammed shut. He couldn't believe what had happened. And he also couldn't believe that Chang had forgotten to bind his hand back up!

Noah jumped into action. He untied his left arm and then his legs. He untangled himself from the cords and dashed to the door. Locked. Noah frantically scanned the room, searching for an escape. Nothing but four padded walls, no windows, no air ducts.

"Think," Noah chided himself. He chewed his lower lip. "Wait. They're sending someone for me."

Noah snatched the cord from the floor, his mind already forming a plan. He lashed one end of the cord to the table leg. He looped the other end around his hand and crouched on the floor next to the door. He pulled the cord taut, holding it about six inches from the floor. He didn't have long to wait.

A few minutes later, the door opened. Dave 'The Wrench' Dixon entered the room, his eyes focused on the chair and table, not the floor. Just as he realized that

Noah was not sitting in the chair, his right foot tripped on the cord. He stumbled forward. Noah tugged the cord up. Dave's other foot became entangled in the cord. He fell hard, striking his head on the edge of the table. He yelped as he hit the floor, then lay still.

Noah closed the door, but left it unlatched so he could get out. He scrambled over and pounced on Dave. He took the cord and tied Dave's hands behind him. Noah grabbed the remaining cord and bound his feet. Satisfied that Dave was firmly secured, Noah rolled him over and searched his pockets. He found a cell phone, wallet, and a small switchblade. Noah pocketed the phone and wallet. He pulled off his shirt and using the knife, cut a strip of fabric from the bottom of it. He took the piece and shoved it into Dave's mouth.

"That should keep you," Noah muttered as he put his shirt back on.

He stood up and tiptoed to the door. He opened it a crack and peeked out. He saw no one, and heard nothing. He slipped out of the room and eased the door shut. He hurried along the hall and crept down the stairs. Where were Wright and Chang? And more importantly, where were his parents?

Voices drifted toward him. Noah turned and sprinted the other way. He came to a living room with a high, vaulted ceiling. He bent down and dashed across it.

"Hey, it's the kid!"

Noah turned and recognized the man with the flat

face, who entered from the other side of the room. Noah gave up all pretense of hiding. He ran down another short hallway but there was nowhere to go. He was trapped. Footsteps pounded behind him. At the last second, Noah noticed a door. He flung it open and ran through. He was in a two-car garage. Noah's eyes darted around. A 2-by-4 board leaned against the wall. He grabbed it and jammed one end under the door handle. The handle wiggled as the man tried to open the door, but the board prevented the handle from turning.

"Open the door!" the man yelled.

Noah hurried to a four-wheel all-terrain vehicle. It was similar to the one that he drove on the beach sometimes.

He pounded the seat. "No keys."

Noah looked around. On the other side of the garage were three Kawasaki motorcycles. All had the keys in the ignition. Anthony had taught Noah how to drive a motorcycle, but Anthony had always sat behind Noah, coaching him. Noah hesitated. A pop like a firecracker made him jump. The man with the flat face was shooting at the door! Noah went to the bike. He'd have to drive it without any help.

Noah was about to jump on the closest motorcycle when he saw two spear guns hanging on the wall next to some scuba gear. Noah grabbed a gun and spear. He set them on the seat and mounted the motorcycle, sitting on the gun and spear. He turned the key, switched the fuel valve on, hit the starter button, and the Kawasaki roared to life. His legs were too short to kick up the kickstand, so Noah twisted the throttle and the motorcycle shot out of the garage. Noah glanced over his shoulder. The man had blasted through the door and was running to the other motorcycles.

Noah had no idea where he was. He steered down a long cement driveway and then onto a dirt road lined with palm trees. He hit a bump and careened to the right, almost losing control of the motorcycle. The back wheel spun and then the bike righted itself. Noah sped up. He gritted his teeth and worked to keep from crashing. The motorcycle was heavier than the one he'd learned on, and it was difficult to manage. Wind whipped by his face and dust got in his eyes. When he turned to look back, he saw the man with the flat face gaining on him.

A wood fence lay ahead. The road suddenly veered to the left. Noah couldn't turn the bike in time. He crashed through the fence and into a bunch of mangrove trees. Leaves struck his face. His skin smarted as he kept driving. Then, he broke into the open. Ahead he saw rocks and sand covering the landscape, then the whitecaps of the ocean. Now he knew he was on the north side of the island. He was quickly approaching the cliff face near the cave where he and Anthony had found the box.

The man with the flat face was still close behind, his mouth twisted into a snarl. Noah looked frantically to the left and right. Too many jumbled boulders and trees. He had nowhere to go!

So, Noah made a decision. He gritted his teeth and gunned the throttle. The Kawasaki exploded forward and Noah watched as the azure ocean filled his vision. The motorcycle bounced around on the rough ground, but Noah held on. Then the land disappeared below him. Noah shot out into open space, the Kawasaki's wheels spinning uselessly. Noah felt weightless for a moment. Then he and the Kawasaki plummeted downward.

CHAPTER TEN

DANGEROUS ROCKS

The Kawasaki slammed into the water with a resounding smack, creating a huge splash. The impact knocked Noah off the bike. He hit the water hard, then sank underwater. His lungs cried for air. He kicked hard, propelling himself upward.

Noah's head bobbed out of the water. He sucked in a great lungful of air, then coughed violently. As he caught his breath, he checked himself over. No cuts, no broken bones, but his left shoulder hurt some. He'd been extremely lucky. The speed of the motorcycle had launched it out far enough that he'd missed landing on dangerous rocks along the shore. The water was still shallow, about twenty feet deep. Noah started to swim toward the shoreline when he heard a loud popping sound. He looked up. The man with the flat face was aiming a pistol at him. Crack! Noah instinctively ducked and dove down into the water.

The water distorted his vision, but he saw the Kawasaki lying on its side on the sandy sea floor. Noah spied the spear gun and spear nearby. He swam down and retrieved both. His lungs burned for air and his shoulder throbbed. He pushed off against the sea floor and shot to the surface.

The man was scanning the water. He saw Noah and aimed the pistol at him.

Noah submerged again, but this time, he swam to the north, away from the cliff. When he needed oxygen again, he surfaced. The man was focused back to the south. But he turned and saw Noah again. He aimed again. Noah didn't hear the shot this time, but he heard the whapping sound as the bullet pierced the water nearby.

Noah twisted away from the shore, trying to get out of range of the gun. His progress was slow because he was carrying the spear gun, and his shoulder ached. After a moment, Noah realized he wasn't hearing gunshots. He turned around and treaded water. The man was talking into a walkie-talkie. Noah waited, catching his breath. Then he heard a sound, a high-pitched hum, interrupted by a whacking sound. It came closer.

Noah turned around. A man on a jet ski was bounding toward him. Noah dove under the water. His body jostled viciously in the surf as the Jet Ski passed over him. Noah kicked, forcing himself downward. He peered up through the rippling water. The Jet Ski was turning around. Noah thought frantically. If he went farther out to sea, he would eventually tire out. Then he would be a sitting duck for the Jet Ski. He made a quick decision, pushing toward the shore.

Noah's lungs craved oxygen. He floated to the surface, not far from the Jet Ski. The man saw him and turned in a loop, barreling down on him again. Noah gulped some air and dove under again. This time he swam as quickly as he could toward the rocky reef along the shore. He was working against the current and fighting panic. He could not keep avoiding the Jet Ski.

Noah had to surface. His head bobbed up and he sucked in air again. The Jet Ski came at him, engine revving hard. Noah flailed with his legs, twisting downward. The underside of the Jet Ski hit his foot. He screamed in pain, air bubbles rising around him. Just before he floated up, Noah realized he was near an outcropping of rocks that was below the surface. He could hide there.

The Jet Ski zoomed by, nearly hitting him again. Noah thrashed in the waves and swallowed a mouthful of salt water. He spat and coughed. By this time, the Jet Ski was rocketing toward him again. Noah could see the man driving it. He was grimacing evilly at Noah.

Noah took in a lungful of air and dove under. He kicked madly until he reached the rocks. He wrapped his legs around one of them. Gaining his balance, he quickly loaded the spear into the spear gun. He watched above him. The Jet Ski had circled again and was whizzing toward him.

Noah braced himself against another rock. He had

one shot so he had to make it count. The Jet Ski bounced over the water, coming closer. Noah aimed the spear gun. As the Jet Ski passed over him, Noah pulled the trigger. The gun jolted in his hand and the spear cut through the water. It struck the underside of the Jet Ski.

The Jet Ski swirled in a loop, then careened toward the shore. Noah surfaced, gasping for air. He turned around just as the Jet Ski collided into the rocks near the shore. The driver flew into the air, landing on a rock. He rolled over and clutched at his back. Then he lay down. Noah dove under again, but this time he looked up to the cliff. The man with the flat face was shading his eyes, looking at the wreckage of the Jet Ski.

Noah dropped the spear gun and swam toward the cliff. When he reached the shore, he ducked in between the rocks, hidden from the man up above. The rocky reef covered a large area off the shore, with outcroppings jutting into the air here and there. Noah moved forward carefully, fighting the current. He edged on and soon he could now touch the sand with his feet. He rested for just a moment with his head above water. He was exhausted and his shoulder hurt. Fish darted around as Noah picked his way through the rocks. When he arrived at the cliff face, he stopped and listened. The man was above him about twenty feet.

The cliff face was rough, with rocky outcroppings and ledges. Noah studied it for a moment. He thought he could climb it. He quickly kicked off the tennis shoes and pulled off his socks. He grasped a rock and hauled himself up. Water dripped from his body and his clothes stuck heavily to his skin. He put a bare foot into a toehold and pushed on. He wasn't sure what he would do once he got to the top, but he didn't want to stay in the water. More than halfway up, he heard the man up above start talking. Noah froze, gripping the rocks with his fingers and toes.

"Georgie's down on a rock. I don't know if he's okay." The man paused, listening. "I don't know where the kid is. He must've drowned." Another moment of silence. "How am I supposed to check on Georgie?" Another long pause. "Fine. I'll climb down. I might break my neck, but fine. Just get a boat out here, too. Okay, I'll meet you down there."

By now Noah was less than ten feet from the top. He could hear the man pacing above him, muttering.

"He must think I'm crazy. I can't climb down there."

Noah scrambled up the last few feet. His head was now just below the top of the cliff. He could see tufts of grass growing at the cliff's edge. He could almost reach out and grab a small tree branch. The man sidled up to the edge of the cliff. Noah could see the tip of his boot.

"How am I gonna do this?" the man said to himself. He cursed. "It's either this or face the boss."

He turned around and got on his knees. He slid his body down and lowered a foot right past Noah's face.

The foot flopped around, trying to find a purchase.

Noah grabbed the man's pant leg and yanked as hard as he could. He almost lost his balance, but he was more fortunate than the man.

"Yaaaaahhh," the man screamed as he fell past Noah. He flayed his arms out, snatching at air. He hit the water with a splatter, miraculously missing any rocks. He floated to the surface, flinging hair out of his face. He sputtered for a second.

Noah crawled the last few feet up the cliff. Sand and dirt stuck to his wet clothes. The rough rocks hurt his bare feet, but he ignored the pain. He jumped to his feet and looked over the edge. The man was treading water, spitting and coughing.

"I'll get you, you little punk!" he yelled at Noah. He pulled his cell phone from his pocket, opened it, then realized it was dead. He threw it up at Noah. It bounced harmlessly on the cliff face.

Noah ran to the man's motorcycle. The key was stuck in the ignition. Noah hopped on and started the bike. He could still hear the man hollering from below as the engine roared to life. Noah cranked the throttle and the bike leaped forward. He drove back over the rocks to the broken fence. Once he was on the dirt road, he sped down the path, back to Isaiah Wright's house.

CHAPTER ELEVEN

THE DONZI

As Noah approached the Wright house, he cut the engine on the motorcycle. It coasted for a few feet, then Noah guided it into a clump of oak trees at the edge of the long driveway. He dismounted and leaned the bike against a tree trunk. Low, spreading branches of a tree hid Noah and the motorcycle. He listened for noise, then poked his head around the branches and watched the house. No one seemed to be about. Wright and his men were either in the house, or had gone to find the man with the flat face and his companion.

Noah ducked under the oak branches and raced up the driveway. He rushed into the garage, breathless. He paused by the ATV. No one had seen him. He strode to the door and quietly opened it. He heard nothing so he slipped into the house. He pressed himself against the wall. Cool air enveloped him, chilling his wet clothes, but Noah didn't notice. He was too focused on finding his parents. He had to get them off Wright's island.

Faint voices interrupted the silence. Noah crept down the hallway to the living room. He paused just before entering the room.

"His parents will give us the exact location of the emerald, I assure you."

Isaiah Wright was speaking!

Goose bumps ran up Noah's arms as he heard Wright talking. Noah peeked around the corner. Wright and another man were sitting in leather wing-back chairs in a large second-floor loft that looked down on the living room. The other man was in jeans and a black tee shirt. Even from a distance, Noah could tell that the man was strong and athletic, with thick biceps and large hands. Chang leaned against a railing, observing them.

Noah hadn't noticed the loft before because he'd been too busy running from the man with the flat face. Noah studied the layout of the living room. He had no way of crossing it without being seen. He knelt down and listened.

"You didn't need to resort to kidnapping," the other man said. "My team would've found the emerald on our own."

Wright chuckled. "Max, your team has done nothing so far, and we didn't have any more time. I had to take matters into my own hands."

Wright was talking to Max Scheff! Noah had never actually seen Max before, he'd just heard his parents describe Max's exploits. As Noah observed Max, he agreed with what his parents had said. He did indeed look like a formidable foe.

"And you'll take the fall for this," Max said.

"What does that mean?"

Max stood up. He ran a hand through his curly brown hair. "I had nothing to do with the Winters, or their kid. I just locate valuables." Max held up his hands. "And then I sell them to the highest bidder."

Isaiah Wright's face came into Noah's view. His eyes narrowed and Noah could feel the hate emanating from them. He approached Max. "I am paying you to find the emerald."

Max shook his head. "At one point, that was true. But I have a higher bidder."

"Who?"

"I can't tell you that," Max said. "But this person will pay a million more than you."

Wright stepped closer to Max, backing him up to the railing. Max glanced over his shoulder. Noah pulled his head back, not breathing.

"You can't intimidate me," Max continued.

Noah looked slowly around the corner again. Max had moved away from the railing. He stood, legs apart, arms crossed, staring at Wright.

Wright tapped his fingers together thoughtfully. "Okay," he finally said. "Let's find the emerald and we will renegotiate a price."

"A million more," Max said. "That's the new price."

Wright walked over to an enormous mahogany

desk. He opened a drawer, pulled out a box, and took something from it.

"Do you see this?" Wright held up a small glass vial.

Max shrugged. "What is it?"

"It's a new poison." Wright lifted the vial up to the light. "It's odorless, tasteless, and untraceable. Just a small injection will kill a person. No autopsy in the world will detect it. I had it specially designed."

"Sure," Max said sarcastically. "What are you, some kind of villain out of a spy story? Trying to threaten me with a new poison."

Wright pursed his lips. "I am no villain. I just get what I want. You should keep that in mind."

"Oh, I will," Max said. "I –"

Wright's cell phone rang. "Yes?" he answered. Wright listened for a moment, then slammed the phone shut.

"That was Karl, my third in command, after Chang here. It seems that young Noah Winter has escaped," Wright said. "Your men can do nothing right."

"What happened?" Max asked.

"Noah attacked Dave when he came to get the boy. The kid ran into the garage and took off on a motorcycle. I don't know how, but two of your men ended up in the ocean. Karl has them now." Wright waved a hand angrily at Max. "Get out there and take care of this."

Max hurried down the stairs, grumbling about his incompetent partners. Noah scooted across the floor and hid behind a long couch. Max stomped through the living room and down the hallway where Noah had just been. Noah breathed a sigh of relief. Once Max was gone, he stared back up into the loft.

Wright was twisting the vial in his fingers. "Chang, our Mr. Scheff thinks he can threaten me."

"Not very smart," Chang said.

"No, it's not." Wright examined the vial. "Once his team finds the emerald, we'll test out this new poison. I think Mr. Scheff will be a perfect candidate, don't you?"

Chang smiled. "Absolutely."

Wright placed the vial back in the box. He turned to Chang. "We'd better go check on things. Max's team may be great at underwater exploration, but they have no idea how to subdue a young boy."

Chang came down the stairs, followed by Wright. They walked across the living room and into the hallway. Wright stopped and opened a door.

"Paul, how are things going?"

Paul's the man guarding my parents! Noah thought.

"Everything's fine," Paul's deep voice boomed from inside the room. "The Winters are quite cooperative now."

"We're doing what you asked," another voice said.

That was his dad! Noah shook with anger. *Wright better not have hurt them,* Noah thought.

"Thank you, Mr. Winter," Wright said. "Once this business is out of the way, we'll reunite you with your son."

Noah heard his dad's muffled voice, but this time he couldn't understand him.

"Get me the information I need and you'll see your son." Wright pulled the door closed. He turned to Chang. "Once they tell us where the emerald is located, the Winters can be the next candidates for the new poison. After Max, of course."

He and Chang disappeared down the hallway.

Noah bit his lip. He had to rescue his parents, or they would all die. But how? He had to get rid of the guard, Paul.

Noah raised his head and looked around. He was alone. Besides the couch, the living room had floor-to-ceiling bookcases, a square coffee table, end tables, and planters that contained bamboo trees. Could he use one of the planters to knock Paul out?

Noah examined a planter. It was made out of thick pottery. He tried to pull the bamboo tree out of the planter, but he couldn't. His eyes roved around the room where his gaze fell on a ceramic lamp with a round marble base sitting on one of the end tables. He picked it up, feeling its weight. That marble base was heavy, but he could lift it.

This should do the trick, he thought.

Noah unplugged the lamp, ripped off the lampshade, and lugged the lamp to the door of the room where his parents were held. He hefted the lamp up, resting it on his shoulder like a baseball bat. He ignored the pain in his shoulder as he knocked on the door.

Paul's low voice filtered out through the crack under the door. "Don't move while I answer the door."

Footsteps clunked on the floor. Noah took a deep breath and braced himself.

"Yeah?" Paul said when he opened the door.

Noah raised the lamp up as high as he could. Paul stuck his head out the door and Noah swung the lamp. The heavy marble end smashed into the side of Paul's head.

"Argh!" he groaned, slumping to the floor. A trickle of blood oozed out of a cut on his forehead. He kicked a foot out and then lay still.

Noah dropped the lamp. It hit the floor with a thump. Noah jumped over Paul and into the room. His mom was sitting at a table, holding a piece of paper. His dad sat next to her, his jaw open in disbelief.

"Noah!" they both shouted, leaping to their feet.

Noah ran into their arms. "Mom! Dad!" he cried. They huddled together for a moment, too happy to say anything.

"How did you –" his mom began, but lost her voice. She hugged Noah again. "You're all wet! Look at your cheek." She brushed a hand over the bruise from Dave's wrench. "What happened?"

"Mom, I'm fine," Noah said.

"He is," Frank agreed as he collected himself. "Let's get out of here."

"Where are Wright and the others?" Riley asked Noah.

"They went to the north end of the island," Noah said. "I don't know if anyone else is around."

Frank crossed to the door and peeked out. "The coast is clear."

"Let's go," Noah said.

Frank held up a hand. He bent down and placed a finger on Paul's neck. "He's still breathing, just knocked out cold." He grabbed Paul's legs and pulled him into the room.

"Come on," Frank waved for Noah to follow him.

"Wait." Riley hurried to the table and rifled through maps, books, and papers. "Here we go." She held up the spyglass with the etched-glass end pieces attached to it. "No sense leaving this with Wright."

"Good idea," Frank said. He pushed her and Noah out the door, pulled it shut and made sure it locked.

They ran out through the living room, down a hallway, and into a large foyer.

"Hold on a second." Frank pointed to a phone on a credenza next to the front door. He picked up the receiver and dialed. "Anthony. Yes, yes, we're fine. I'll explain later. Get the *Explorer* and head out to Copper Key. Don't worry, we'll find you, just get out here as fast as you can!"

"What are we going to do?" Noah whispered as they crept out the front door.

"Let's see if there's a boat we can take," Frank said. "Hurry up."

They ran down a stone path, past a gazebo to a dock where two sleek boats were moored. Frank hopped into a two-seater 388 Slingshot powerboat.

"I'll see if I can disable this so they can't follow us," he said. "Riley," he gestured at the other boat, a dark blue and white Donzi powerboat. "Get that started."

Riley jumped into the Donzi, tucking the spyglass in her arm. She sat behind the wheel and fired up the engine. Noah followed her, but leaned over the side to watch Frank in the other boat.

Frank opened a hatch, exposing the engine. "I need something to cut the fuel line."

Noah felt in his pocket. He'd forgotten all about the knife he'd taken from Dave 'The Wrench' Dixon. "Here," he said, pulling out the knife and tossing it to his dad.

Frank raised his eyebrows in surprise as he caught the knife. He flicked open the blade and cut the fuel line. Dark liquid dripped out of the tiny tube.

"That ought to do it," he said. He leaped over the side of the Slingshot and into the Donzi.

Noah looked up. Off to the north, another Slingshot speedboat bounded over the water, speeding toward them like a rocket. "They're back!" he hollered.

"Get the line," Frank pointed at the rope line that tied the Donzi to the dock. Noah grabbed the rope and freed the boat. "Go!" Frank yelled to Riley.

Riley pushed the accelerator and the boat vaulted away from the dock.

The Slingshot was about thirty feet from them. Wright was at the wheel. Chang stood in a half-crouch, ready for action.

Frank gestured wildly at Riley. "Try to outrun them."

Riley sped up, but the Slingshot veered at them. The other boat had momentum and quickly barreled down on the Donzi. Riley yanked the wheel to the right. Wright's boat glanced off the Donzi's side. The spyglass fell to the bottom of the boat and rolled around wildly on the floor.

"Get it!" she yelled at Noah.

Noah scrambled after the spyglass, but it spun away from him. He crawled after it, finally snatching it up. He sat back in a chair and held on tightly to the spyglass.

As the two boats clanged together, Chang hurdled over the side of the Slingshot and landed right in front of them. He wavered for a moment, trying to catch his balance. Frank sprung at Chang and hit him in the face.

Chang merely shook his head, as if he'd been smacked with a flyswatter. He took a step forward.

"Is that the best you have?" he snarled at Frank.

Frank raised his fist and swung at Chang again. This time, Chang grabbed Frank's fist, crushing it in his own hand.

"Ah!" Frank grimaced. He backed away, staggering as the boat rocked in the choppy waves. Then he fell to his knees.

The Donzi picked up speed as Noah's mom revved the engine. Behind it, Wright's Slingshot kept pace with the Donzi.

Chang advanced on Frank. He hauled Frank to his feet. Frank grappled with Chang, both faltering with the wobbly motion of the boat. Frank managed to push Chang back a foot. Noah saw his opportunity. He dove to the bottom of the boat behind Chang. Riley glanced back and saw where Noah was. She jerked the wheel, which caused Chang to stumble. He backed up and bumped heavily into Noah. Noah pushed sideways and Chang's feet flew into the air. He lurched back, grabbing onto Frank's shirt, and pulled Frank with him as he tumbled over the side of the boat.

"Dad!" Noah shouted. He dropped the spyglass on the floor.

Riley glanced over her shoulder again. "Frank!" She cut the power to the boat.

Frank threw out an arm and clung to the side of the

boat, his feet dragging in the water behind him. Frank's shirt ripped where Chang had grabbed hold, and Chang fell into the water. He kicked about, flailing violently in the wake of the boat. Wright nearly ran him over as he pursued the Donzi.

Noah grabbed Frank by the back of his jeans and helped him crawl into the boat.

"Keep going!" Frank yelled at Riley. She accelerated and the Donzi whizzed through the water. "Where's the spyglass?"

Noah looked around frantically.

"There it is." He seized the spyglass from under a chair.

"Don't let go of it!" Frank ordered him. "Stay in the bottom of the boat where you're safe."

Noah hunkered down on his knees, still high enough where he could watch what was happening.

Behind them, Wright had circled his boat around and stopped for Chang. The Slingshot had lost distance, but Wright was not giving up, and the Slingshot slowly gained on the Donzi.

Noah, Frank, and Riley all gazed ahead, searching for the *Explorer*. Noah turned and looked back. Wright's boat was getting closer.

"Come on," Riley muttered to the Donzi, her hands gripping the wheel tightly.

The Donzi cut through the water, jarring them as it hit wave after wave. Noah glanced back again. The

Slingshot drew nearer. What would happen if Wright overtook them? Noah thought about Wright and the vial of poison. He shuddered.

"Frank, I can't go any faster," Riley shouted.

"We'll have to lose them somehow," Frank hollered back.

"We won't make it!" Riley gritted her teeth.

And then they saw the *Explorer*.

CHAPTER TWELVE

THE FLOUR SIFTER

The *Explorer* approached on the horizon and its horn sounded loudly. Nearby Noah spotted a police cruiser.

"It's Chief Burton!" Noah jumped up and down and waved his hands.

Behind them, Wright's boat slowed down.

"They see the police," Frank said. "Wright's giving up."

Wright made a U-turn and sped off, vanishing from view.

Riley guided the Donzi up to the *Explorer*. The police cruiser drew up alongside both. The *Explorer*'s engine stopped.

Anthony bounded out of the cabin. "You're all right!" he shouted joyfully.

Riley killed the Donzi's engine. "We're fine, thanks to Noah."

Anthony helped Noah climb from the Donzi to the *Explorer*. Riley almost fell into the water as she followed Noah.

"After all we've been through, I almost take a dunk into the ocean!" she laughed as she dropped into a seat.

Chief Burton emerged from the cabin of the police cruiser. Detective Shaw appeared behind him. Both had stern looks on their faces.

"Noah, what in the world were you thinking?" Chief Burton said. "Anthony told us all about your plans to meet the kidnappers without the police, and that you had disappeared." He shook his head. "We searched all around Marquesas Keys but couldn't find you. I can't tell you all how relieved I am to see you."

"Isaiah Wright kidnapped us," Noah blurted out.

Chief Burton wrinkled his brow. "What happened?" he asked Frank, who was still in the Donzi.

"After we left the station the other night, we headed back to our house," Frank said. "On the way home, I saw an accident on the road. It looked like a motorcycle had crashed and a man was lying in the road. I figured he was hurt, so I got out to help. But someone jumped me from behind. Whoever it was put a rag to my face and that's all I remember."

"Someone did the same to me," Riley said. "I was just getting out of the car myself when someone covered my nose with a rag."

"Probably chloroform," Chief Burton said. "Simple to do."

"Next thing we know, we're tied up in a room,"

Frank continued. "We didn't know what happened to the car or Noah. Then a man we didn't recognize took us to a room filled with books and maps, like a large library. He gave us the spyglass, and told us to figure out where the De La Rosa Emerald was hidden."

"We just made up the location," Riley interrupted. "We still haven't figured out what the map really says."

Frank nodded. "We had to stall for time until we could figure out a way to escape."

"But then he captured Noah and threatened to hurt him," Riley said.

"Who?" Chief Burton frowned.

"Isaiah Wright," Noah replied.

"And how did Isaiah Wright get a hold of you?" Chief Burton asked Noah. He leaned his knees against the side of the boat and put his hands on his hips. "Why didn't you and Anthony let the police handle things? You could've been killed."

"We'd like to know that, too," Riley said. "We were too busy getting away from Wright to hear what happened to you."

"I'm sorry," Noah said to Chief Burton. "I didn't think that a stand-in would fool the kidnappers, so Anthony and I decided we would go by ourselves."

Then Noah turned to his parents. His words tumbled over each other as he explained all that had occurred since his parents' disappearance.

"That's quite a story," Chief Burton said when

Noah finished. He stared off on the horizon. "Isaiah Wright's behind all this."

"Yes," Noah said.

Chief Burton pursed his lips. "That man's a billionaire. He's involved in all kinds of philanthropic endeavors. He's odd, no doubt, but I never would've thought he'd be capable of this."

"He is," Frank said.

Chief Burton sucked in a breath and let it out slowly. "You all need to come into the station and make a statement," he said.

"We can't do that right now," Frank replied.

"What?" Detective Shaw glared at Frank. "Do you want to let that man get away with kidnapping?"

"Of course not," Frank snapped. "But I – "

"Frank, I'm your friend and neighbor, but I'm also Chief of Police," Chief Burton interrupted. "You have to make an official report about what happened."

Frank waved him off. "Ben, we will, but right now we have to find the De La Rosa Emerald. Max Scheff and Wright are after it, just like we are. We've got to find the emerald before they do, or all of this will be for nothing. We'll come in and make a statement once we have the emerald."

"Please, Ben," Riley said. "I can't tell you how important finding the emerald is."

Chief Burton gazed out into the water, thinking. Then he turned to Detective Shaw. "Let's go out to

Copper Key and have a talk with Mr. Wright."

"What about their statements?" Detective Shaw asked.

"We can't force them to make a report if they don't want to," Chief Burton said. "And I know Frank and Riley." Chief Burton's mouth curled into a smile. "Once they're after some lost treasure, nothing will stop them. Not even the Chief of Police. The Winters can come in to the station later and we'll get their statements then. Right now, we'll visit Isaiah Wright."

"He won't tell you anything," Frank said.

"Of course not," Chief Burton snorted. "He's too smart to let himself get caught in anything. I'm sure he's removed any traces of your presence there. I doubt I could find even part of a fingerprint, let alone a soundproofed room or other evidence of foul play. Not only that, I don't have a warrant to search the house. What I will do is tow the Donzi back there and ask Wright how it came into your possession. And he can explain why he was following you. I suspect he'll say you were trespassing on his island and that you stole the Slingshot to escape, and they were just trying to get the boat back."

"That's a lie," Noah said.

"Yes, it is." Chief Burton held up his hands. "I should be able to get a warrant to search his house. But unless I can find proof that he kidnapped you, there's not a lot I can do."

"Thanks, Ben," Frank said. "Let's tie up the Donzi." He helped Chief Burton and Detective Shaw secure a line from the police cruiser to the Donzi. Then Frank leaped across into the *Explorer*. "I'll stop by later on tonight to give you an update."

"I'm counting on it," Chief Burton said. "And for you to make a statement when you complete your treasure hunt."

"You have our word," Riley said.

"What about Wright?" Noah asked. "Will he try to hurt us again?"

Chief Burton shook his head. "He knows we're on to him, so he'll have to be careful."

"We'll be careful, too," Riley said, patting Noah's shoulder. "No more excitement for us."

But that was not to be.

***

Against Noah's protests, Frank and Riley took him to the hospital to have his shoulder examined. Luckily, Noah suffered no broken bones or pulled muscles. Noah's shoulder was bruised, but the doctor in the emergency room assured everyone that in a few days, the shoulder would feel fine.

Back at the Winters' house, Riley and Anthony fixed sandwiches for everyone. While they ate, Noah and his parents chatted excitedly about everything that had happened to them. Juan Carlo and Anthony sat on the edge of their chairs, enthralled by the story.

"Increíble," Juan Carlo murmured repeatedly while they talked.

"Now Wright and Max have the map," Frank said in conclusion. "We had to show it to them."

"It's just a matter of time before they figure out what the map means," Riley said.

"But they're missing the cross piece, just like we are," Noah said.

"What do you mean?" Frank asked.

"We're missing another piece," Noah replied.

"There should be a piece that attaches to the etched pieces of glass," Juan Carlo said. "It has lines to mark the exact spot where the emerald is hidden."

"'X' marks the spot," Noah said.

Frank shrugged. "Even so, we're still not sure what part of the Keys the map is showing."

"We traced the map onto paper," Anthony said. "But we couldn't figure it out either."

Frank stood up. "Let's project the map up onto the wall."

Riley had put the spyglass in a safe when they'd returned home. She retrieved it and gave it to Anthony. He held it up and Riley shone a flashlight through the end of it.

"We found notches on the edges of the glass pieces," Anthony said.

"So we lined up the notches, like this." Noah reached around his mother and rotated the glass pieces so the notches pointed toward the ceiling. "This way, the arrow on the map points to the north."

Noah twisted the glass pieces slightly until the lines on the wall resembled a map of islands.

Frank rubbed his chin as he studied the map. "I have no idea what group of islands those are." He scrunched up his face. "Or even if that's a set of islands in the Keys."

"It doesn't look like anything to me," Riley said.

"Let's get back to the cross piece." Anthony set the spyglass back on the table. "Juan Carlo, do you know what it looks like?"

"It's supposed to be made of porcelain," Juan Carlo said. "It's round and fits over the other two etched-glass pieces. It's got wires hooked in it, like the crosshairs in a rifle scope." Juan Carlo took a piece of paper from the table and drew a circle and lines. "Like this."

"If it wasn't with the glass pieces that we found in the cave, it must've been kept with the spyglass," Anthony said.

"That means it's somewhere around the *San Isabel* wreckage," Frank said.

Riley scowled. "Unless Alfonso De La Rosa hid it someplace else."

All of a sudden, Noah's mind flashed back to when they'd dived the *San Isabel* earlier that week. He remembered the circular piece of porcelain he found. He'd thought it was a flour sifter. Now he knew it wasn't. "I found that piece," he said.

They all looked at him in surprise.

"Where is it?" Riley finally asked.

"I don't have it now," Noah replied.

"What?" Frank jumped up. "What did you do with it?"

Noah shrugged sheepishly. "Remember when we were exploring the *San Isabel* on Tuesday? I told you I found something by the ship? Well, when that shark swam out of the hole in the hull and startled me, I dropped it."

"Oh no!" Riley slumped down in her chair.

"I thought it was a flour sifter or something," Noah explained. "I didn't think it was important or I would've told you."

"It's okay," Frank said. "We'll have to go find it now."

"Now?" Juan Carlo asked. "It's almost dark."

Frank nodded. "We've done plenty of night dives. We'll take the underwater lights and we've got a spotlight on the *Explorer* that will help illuminate the shipwreck." He turned to Noah. "You dropped the piece by that jagged hole, right? Up near the bow?"

"Yes," Noah said.

"Let's go!" Anthony hopped to his feet.

CHAPTER THIRTEEN

X MARKS THE SPOT

The sun had set by the time the *Explorer* approached the dive site. Stars dotted the night sky, and the water was dark as oil.

"Noah, you'll show us where you were when you dropped the porcelain piece," Riley said. "Anthony, you stay with Juan Carlo on board the *Explorer*. I doubt Wright or Max Scheff will try anything, but if you run into problems, kill the spotlight. Then we'll know you're in trouble."

"That'll work," Anthony said.

Frank dived into the water, followed by Riley. Their underwater flashlights twinkled in the dark depths. Noah jumped off the back of the boat, quickly sinking beneath the ocean's surface. The spotlight from the *Explorer* faded into a yellowy haze. He couldn't see much beyond what the beam of his light illuminated. Off to his left and right, there was nothing but darkness. Noah kicked hard, joining his parents as they swam toward the *San Isabel*. His shoulder ached as he swam, but he gritted his teeth and didn't let it slow him down.

Frank gestured for Noah to join him. Noah swam up beside his dad, coming to the hole in the port side of the ship. Noah moved to where he had been when his dad had surprised him and he'd dropped the piece of porcelain. Noah descended down to the ocean floor.

Further above them, the light from the *Explorer*'s spotlight illuminated the top of the shipwreck in a hazy glow. Shadows danced off the side of the shipwreck. But on the ocean floor, it was almost completely dark. Noah thought of an underwater haunted house.

It's spooky down here, he thought, shaking off an uneasy feeling.

His mom and dad joined him. They felt around on the ocean floor, stirring up sand. Riley lifted up a hand and waved something around. Noah took the object from her, then shook his head. They kept searching.

Noah paused for a few seconds, trying to picture the object as it slowly settled into the sand. He thought about what he had been doing. He wasn't motionless when the shark startled him. He'd been kicking his feet to stay by the ship's hull. So the water around him had been moving. Maybe the porcelain piece hadn't floated straight down. Maybe it had floated off sideways. Noah moved alongside the bottom of the shipwreck, one hand holding his flashlight, the other hand feeling in the sand. He touched some rocks and coral, then something else. He lifted up his hand. In it was the round porcelain piece with the two wires!

He swam over to his parents, elated.

Riley nodded her head when she saw him holding the piece. Through her face mask, Noah saw the excitement in her eyes. Frank pointed with his thumb for them to surface.

Noah spit out his regulator as soon as he surfaced. "Found it!" he shouted, holding the porcelain ring up.

Frank and Riley swam over and inspected the piece in the moonlight.

"The wire pieces aren't aligned like Juan Carlo's drawing," Noah said. "See? The wires don't cross in the center of the circle. They cross over to one side." The porcelain piece looked like this:

"That's okay," Frank said. "As long as we correctly line this up with the other glass pieces, I'm sure it'll tell us where the emerald is."

"Did you find it?" Anthony leaned over the side of the boat.

"Yes, Noah found it!" Riley said as they swam over to the *Explorer*.

"This is excellent," Juan Carlo said as he helped them aboard. He took the porcelain ring from Noah. "Now we have all the pieces for the spyglass. How amazing!"

"Anthony, head us back to shore," Frank said as he

took off his wet suit. "We've got to put this piece on the spyglass and see what we have."

"Aye, aye, captain," Anthony said, saluting Frank with a grin.

***

"Let's try this again," Anthony said an hour later.

Everyone was sitting in the Winters' living room, watching Anthony. He had attached the etched-glass pieces to the spyglass, and then he twisted on the porcelain piece, lining up the notches so the map displayed correctly. Riley turned on a flashlight, shining the beam through the spyglass. An image appeared on the wall.

"That doesn't look like anything," Frank said. "That crosspiece points to the ocean."

"This can't be right." Riley fiddled with the porcelain piece. "We must not be lining this up correctly."

Frank and Anthony shook their heads as they stared at the map on the wall. "No, that still doesn't make sense."

While they talked, Noah got up and went to his dad's office. He returned a moment later with a powerful magnifying glass.

"May I look at those pieces?" he asked.

"Sure." Anthony handed him the spyglass.

"What are you thinking?" Frank asked Noah.

"Look how small the etching on the glass is,"

Noah replied. "Whoever made this had to use a magnifying glass to etch a map so tiny. What if he put other writing on the porcelain piece or the glass that's so small you have to enlarge it in order to see it?"

"Hey, that makes sense!" Frank nodded.

"What a smart boy," Juan Carlo said.

Noah blushed. "Let's see if I'm right." He peered through the magnifying glass. "Here, on the edge of the glass pieces. There's a tiny 'N' on each one of them." He handed the magnifying glass to Riley.

She examined the edge of the glass. "How about that," she murmured.

"'N' for North," Juan Carlo said.

Noah took the magnifying glass back from his mom. "And look here," Noah continued. "Painted onto the edge of the porcelain piece is a small arrow. I didn't see it before."

Riley stared at him. "You're already a fine treasure hunter."

"I wonder what the arrow means?" Noah said. He pocketed the magnifying glass and twisted the end pieces on the spyglass, lining up the 'N's until each one pointed toward the ceiling. He held the spyglass up and Riley shined the light through it again.

"Okay, but what islands are those?" Anthony said. "There are over seventeen hundred islands in the Keys."

"And look at the arrow on the map," Riley said. "It's pointing to the East."

"And the crossbeam from the porcelain still points into the ocean," Frank said.

"Maybe that's where Alfonso hid the emerald?" Juan Carlo asked skeptically.

"Wait," Noah said. "I'll bet the arrow on the porcelain piece matches the arrow on the glass." He turned the porcelain ring so that the ring lined up with the arrow on the map, pointing due East.

"Look at that." Frank said slowly, with awe in his voice.

The cross pieces now laid over the southwest edge of a large area on the map.

"X marks the spot," Noah said.

Riley moved over to the wall and put a finger on the map in the center of the crosshairs. "This is where we're supposed to look."

"Increíble," Juan Carlo whispered.

"But that doesn't even look like it's pointing to an island," Frank said. "If I had to guess, that's somewhere in the Everglades."

The Everglades are subtropical wetlands covering most of the southern portion of Florida. So much water covers the area that the Everglades are only navigable by boat or canoe. The 'Glades, as they are locally known, have large sawgrass prairies, dark watery woodlands, and labyrinths of swamps, lagoons, and creeks.

Noah turned to Juan Carlo. "Is there anything more in Alfonso's journal?"

"Alfonso wrote a journal?" Frank turned to Juan Carlo.

Juan Carlo reddened. "I'm afraid I kept this from you." He explained to Frank and Riley about the existence of the journal. "But that is in the past," he said as he saw Frank frown at him. Juan Carlo went into the guest bedroom off and returned with Alfonso's journal. "I've read this thing so many times, but I don't believe Alfonso mentions anything that would be of help to us."

Juan Carlo hummed to himself as he carefully turned pages in the old journal. "Here's something about the *San Isabel*, but that doesn't help us," he mumbled. "Ah, I know Alfonso wrote something about a house that Roberto De La Rosa stayed at." Juan Carlo flipped to a different page in the journal, running his hand lightly over the writing. "Here it is. Roberto stayed at a place called 'Paso del Caimán'." He looked up. "Does anyone know where that is?"

"That was almost two hundred years ago," Riley said. "Who knows where that place was."

"What's that mean in English?" Noah asked.

"The, uh, what is the word?" Juan Carlo struggled with the translation. "The Hole of the Alligator?"

"Oh, I know what it is," Anthony said. "The 'Pass of the Alligator', like a mountain pass."

"Yes." Juan Carlo smiled. "I think that would be correct."

Anthony smirked. "And my mother said I'd never

use my high school Spanish."

"There aren't any mountains or mountain passes in Florida," Frank said wryly.

"Wait a minute," Noah snapped his fingers. "I just read about that." He rifled through the books on the coffee table. "I think it was in this one." He lifted up the book about pirates that he'd been reading a few days earlier.

He flipped pages for a moment, then began reading. "Smuggler's Den, once known as 'The Alligator Gap', was a place where pirates stayed in southern Florida. Located deep in the Florida Everglades, the site was a perfect place for pirates to hide out. The pirates built a house to survive the rainy season. The house had a huge stone fireplace and three lookout towers built into the cypress trees. The famous pirate Blackbeard was rumored to have stayed there. In the 1970's, this same place was used by drug smugglers. Small airplanes would drop packages of drugs into the Everglades, and drug runners would retrieve the parcels. Since Smuggler's Den is extremely difficult to find, drug runners stayed there to avoid local law enforcement."

Noah looked up. "What better place to hide an emerald than in a smugglers' den!"

"I knew there was a reason I bought him that book," Riley laughed.

"But why would Roberto De La Rosa stay with pirates?" Noah asked. "Unless he was a pirate himself."

Juan Carlo cleared his throat. "This is most difficult to discuss," he said, his face reddening. "You see, there was a family rumor that Roberto was, in fact, a pirate. He associated with royalty and even worked for the king, so no one suspected that he could be a criminal. It is a dark part of my family's past, one that I always denied. But I suspect that it is true."

"It's okay," Noah said. "It was a long time ago."

"That doesn't matter now," Anthony said. "What we need to know is where on Smuggler's Den would Roberto hide the emerald?" Anthony asked.

"Either in the lookout towers. Or maybe in the chimney," Noah smiled. "Slip out a loose stone, shove the emerald in, and no one knows."

"You could be right," Frank said. "The emerald would be safe until Roberto returned."

"Only he never did," Juan Carlo said.

"But are the towers and fireplace still standing?" Noah wondered.

"Only one way to find out," Frank said. "Find the house."

"But where is it?" Anthony asked.

They all stared at the map on the wall.

"That's not Key West," Riley murmured.

"Maybe it's closer toward Key Largo," Frank suggested.

"That's it!" Noah said. He strode over to the wall and pointed at a spot on the map. "Look, this *is* Key

Largo. See the lines here? This is the edge of the Everglades."

Frank's mouth dropped open. "You're right. Why didn't I see that?"

Noah smiled proudly. "Mom had me studying this the other day."

"Good for her." Frank high-fived Noah.

"This place is somewhere in the Everglades?" Anthony asked.

Riley nodded at the map. "X marks the spot."

CHAPTER FOURTEEN

GHOSTS

As the sun slowly crept across the eastern horizon, the Winters, Anthony and Juan Carlo had made the two-hour drive from Key West. Frank pulled the SUV into a parking place at Scottie's Boat Shop in Everglades City, in Southwestern Florida.

The previous evening, Frank and Riley had decided that the best thing to do was for everyone to get some rest. They planned to rise at dawn and drive up to Everglades City, where they could rent an airboat to find Smuggler's Den. Noah was so excited about finding the De La Rosa emerald that he was sure he wouldn't sleep a wink. But exhaustion overtook him and he was out shortly after his head hit the pillow. He didn't even notice when Indy crawled up onto the bed and laid down next to him.

As they pulled up to the boat shop, Frank said, "Scottie should have a boat for us."

Noah went with his dad and Anthony into Scottie's to rent the airboat. Scottie was a big man and Noah noticed Scottie's large belly hanging over his jeans shorts. He leaned over the counter as he filled out paperwork for the boat rental.

"So where y'all lookin' to go?" Scottie drawled with a Southern twang, his smile stretching across his whole face.

"You ever heard of Smuggler's Den?" Anthony asked.

"Shoot!" Scottie said. "Y'all lookin' for that place? You must be crazy."

"Why is that?" Frank asked as he paid the bill.

"Well, first, it's miles back in the 'Glades," Scottie said, rubbing the stubble on his chin. "And there's ghosts out there."

"Sure." Frank raised an eyebrow. "Old pirates, right?"

Scottie nodded his head emphatically. "You can believe what you want, but my daddy's been out that way, a long time ago. He heard the howls of the ghosts, and he saw spirits walkin' around."

Frank smiled. "I think I'll take my chances."

"Others have," Scottie continued. "And they haven't come back."

"Really?" Anthony asked.

"Yep," Scottie said. "Some teenagers went out there, on a dare. They never came back."

Frank frowned. "I remember that. It was about fifteen years ago."

"Yep." Scottie rubbed his chin again. "And there's

been others."

Frank pushed Noah toward the door. "Let's go."

Anthony stayed behind, talking to Scottie.

"Do you believe him?" Noah asked his dad.

Frank shrugged. "Not enough to stop me from finding the emerald."

"There were a lot of pirates around here," Noah said. "Blackbeard, Lafitte, Gasparilla, Kidd, Rackham, and Bowlegs. Some of them could've died in the Everglades."

"Yes, and their treasures are buried all over southern Florida and in the Keys," Frank said. "But I doubt their ghosts are around. Besides, we survived Isaiah Wright. I think we can handle some old pirate ghosts."

Noah grinned. They waved to his mom and Juan Carlo, who got out of the SUV. Riley carried a backpack with a GPS, waterproof charts of the area, a compass, a guidebook of the Everglades, and other gear that they might need. She also brought the spyglass, just in case Max and his men broke into their house again. Behind her, Juan Carlo followed with a large cooler filled with food and water.

"There's the airboat." Frank led them to a dock where the boat waited. Noah saw their airboat, with its flat bottom and airplane propeller that allowed it to skim above the sawgrass in the Everglades. Frank stepped onto the boat and sat in the elevated seat in the stern, where he could see over the swamp vegetation in the Everglades. Riley and Juan Carlo hopped in and tucked the gear and cooler under the seats. Noah jumped in after them, resting on a seat by the edge of the boat.

"Scottie told me where he thinks Smuggler's Den is," Anthony said as he ran up to join them. "If he's right, it's outside the boundary of Everglades National Park."

"That's good," Frank said. "We don't want to break the law." Juan Carlo looked at him curiously. "If we found the emerald in the national park, we couldn't remove it because it's on federal property," Frank explained.

"I would fight the government for it," Juan Carlo said.

"Good luck with that," Anthony laughed.

"None of that will matter if we don't get going," Riley chided them. "We've got to find the emerald."

"Where to?" Frank asked Anthony.

Anthony got out the charts and the GPS. He and Frank plotted out their course. Riley listened in, but Noah watched other boats leave the dock.

"Earplugs," Frank instructed them. The huge fan on the boat was extremely loud, so they all put earplugs in their ears.

Once everyone was seated, Frank started the engine and navigated away from the dock. Noah's body hummed with the vibration from the fan and engine. The airboat picked up speed and they were soon cutting through the sawgrass, named so because the thick blades were so sharp they could cut through skin. Since the airboat fan was so loud, no one tried to talk. Frank headed inland, steering the boat along a slough, a free-flowing water channel. They watched the foliage on either side of the boat. Noah spotted mangroves and beautiful water lilies. He also saw bladderwort, a carnivorous plant that feeds on water fleas, tadpoles, and mosquito larvae. Noah couldn't believe that the beautiful yellow flowers that looked like snapdragons could actually eat small organisms. Then Noah spied an alligator sunning himself in the tall sawgrass, his skin gunmetal dark.

After a while, they left the other boats behind. Frank turned off the engine and let the boat drift.

"We're getting into the backcountry," he yelled so the others could hear him with their earplugs in. "Now where?"

"The directions are a bit sketchy," Anthony said. "Pinpointing landmarks that Scottie's father described to him is going to be difficult. The GPS isn't going to help us now."

"You don't know exactly where Smuggler's Den is?" Juan Carlo asked.

"We're not really sure," Frank answered. "Two hundred years ago it was supposed to be a small island with a little patch of land, but now, who knows if anything is left. And Scottie at the boat shop says people avoid that area of the 'Glades."

"Why?" Juan Carlo asked.

"Ghosts," Noah said.

"Ghosts?" Juan Carlo repeated.

"Don't worry about it," Frank said. "We'll find the place."

"Even if we locate the site where the pirate house was, if the house has fallen down, we may never find the emerald," Riley said.

"If it's there," Frank said.

As they talked, Noah studied his surroundings. The Everglades were home to many types of birds, alligators, American crocodiles, frogs, turtles, snakes, and much more. Noah glanced up. A red-tailed hawk shrieked, then swooped away into the swamp. Something stirred nearby. Noah spotted a great blue heron. It stood in the water near the sawgrass, staring back at Noah.

"There's a place Scottie called 'Bellows Fork'. It's supposed to be a mile or so farther," Anthony said. "There should be two sloughs on either side of a small island, like a fork in a road. We take the left one."

"If the landscape hasn't changed," Riley said.

Frank shrugged. "I guess we'll see."

No one talked. Off to their left, another alligator slept under a mangrove tree. He raised his head as the boat slid by. Large teeth extended over the sides of his long mouth. "Wow," Noah murmured, in awe of the reptile. Noah knew that an alligator's jaws are so power-ful that their bite could break a man's arm.

Frank revved up the engine and they sped off. Soon the sawgrass prairie became more heavily populated with mangrove and cypress trees. Frank slowed down the boat.

"I think this is our turn-off," he pointed ahead.

Two sloughs flowed around another small island formed out of tropical hardwood hammock.

"Take the left," Riley said. "Just like a treasure map."

Frank steered the boat cautiously through terrain that became denser with foliage. Live oak and other trees overhung the slough. Sunlight flickered through the shadows, dancing off the aluminum boat.

"Now we're looking for an old cypress tree," Anthony said. "It stands alone, which rarely happens in the 'Glades. Past it, we head west into the swamp. There won't be any slough to follow. About a quarter mile inland, there's supposed to be a ground site where the house was built."

"That's pretty vague," Frank said.

Anthony held up his hands. "That's all Scottie said."

"What's a ground site?" Juan Carlo asked.

"It's a place in the Everglades where someone could actually walk on dry land," Frank said. "They're pretty rare. Most of the sites are used by campers."

Riley sighed. "Let's go."

The airboat skimmed across the dark water for several minutes.

"There it is!" Noah shouted.

To the left, a tall cypress stood majestically, away from the other trees in the swamp.

"How far do I go before I head west?" Frank asked.

"I don't know," Anthony said, shrugging. "Scottie just said past the tree."

Frank slowed the airboat down and maneuvered it into a turn. They were now slicing their own path through the Everglades.

Anthony looked ahead. After a moment he held up his hand for Frank to stop. "This should be far enough."

"But I don't see any ground site," Riley said.

"Let's go a little farther," Anthony suggested.

"Sounds good." Frank revved the engine again and the airboat pushed forward.

It was hard to see through the dense forest. Heat and humidity hung around them like a wet blanket. Sweat trickled down Noah's back. He saw another alligator slip into the water. They came to an area thick with trees and shrubs. A breeze rustled the leaves.

"I don't think I can go any farther," Frank said. "The foliage here is too thick."

"Do we have to turn back?" Riley asked, disappointment in her voice.

Something buzzed in Noah's ear and he swatted a mosquito off his cheek.

Frank swiveled the rudders and turned the boat around. As he did so, Noah spotted something through the trees.

"Wait! What's that?" He pointed to the west.

Through the thick branches, something white hung from a tree. It swayed back and forth, an eerie specter hidden in the cypress. Then a tinny, rattling sound wafted over to them.

"What is that?" Frank muttered.

"A ghost?" Juan Carlo fingered a small crucifix hanging around his neck.

"I think there's an island there," Anthony said. "Pull closer."

Frank cut the engine and the boat glided until it struck dry land. Anthony leaped from the boat and dug his way through the foliage. He returned a moment later, holding up a tattered sheet. Dozens of aluminum cans were tied to the fabric.

"Someone tried to make a ghost." Anthony shook the fabric and the cans rattled noisily.

"I'll bet the drug runners put that up to scare people away," Riley said.

"It's not that scary," Noah said.

"Think about it if you were here at nighttime," Anthony said. "This place would be a lot spookier."

"I think we've found the place," Frank said.

Anthony nodded. "It's pretty swampy in there, but it's definitely an island."

Frank started the engine and the airboat drifted slowly away from the land. The boat eased forward through the water. They all focused on the island. Through the thick tree branches a tall structure emerged like a lone skyscraper in the forest.

"Is that it?" Juan Carlo asked.

Before anyone could answer, a low, moaning sound filtered through the trees.

"What was that?" Noah whispered.

Frank and Riley exchanged an uneasy glance.

"Another ghost?" Riley asked skeptically.

"Ghosts can't talk," Frank said.

Noah and Anthony looked around. Juan Carlo touched the crucifix again. The moan came again. Chills ran up Noah's arms.

"Is anyone there?" Frank called out.

Silence.

Riley leaned over the side of the boat, gazing toward the land. "I don't see anyone," she finally said, sitting back down.

Anthony pulled a pair of binoculars from the backpack. He focused through the trees. "I don't see anything that resembles a lookout tower. Wait, what's that?" He paused. "It's a stone fireplace."

"It's still standing," Noah grinned.

"Man, it's leaning badly to one side," Anthony

said. "I'll bet it's sinking into the swamp."

Frank came down from the elevated chair. He and Anthony used oars to push the boat to the edge of the island.

"All I see is tree roots, muck, and water," Frank said as he poked his oar into the grass and brush at the edge of the island.

"Let's see if we can get the boat over to the other side, closer to the chimney," Riley suggested.

"Good idea." Frank started the airboat and navigated through the marsh. As they rounded the island, they could see the stone chimney sticking up through the tree branches like a lighthouse. The house that had been around it had long since fallen down. Frank stopped the boat and they drifted until it clunked against tree roots close to the island.

"There's not much dry land left," Anthony said. "The swamp's overtaken it. We'll have to go through that quagmire to get to the chimney."

Frank handed an oar to Anthony and both pushed the boat through the shallow water.

Noah thought about alligators and snakes. They were out there, lurking in the murky water. He looked around. Did he hear something? He cocked his head, listening.

"What?" Riley asked, noting his anxious expression.

Noah chewed his lip. "I thought maybe I heard

something."

Riley held up a hand and listened intently. She motioned for Frank and Anthony to stop rowing the boat. "I hear it too." Noah saw the veins in her neck ripple with tension.

A high whine seeped over the marsh.

Riley relaxed. "It's just another boat in the area."

"Come on," Frank gestured at Anthony. "Let's find a good place to go ashore."

They pushed hard, edging the boat along the shore of the island. Through the trees, the fireplace came into view. It was over fifteen feet tall, made of large gray stones. It was about ten feet at its base, a solid rectangle about five feet high. But then it narrowed to a tall column. The whole structure tilted precariously to one side.

"Whoever built it must have hauled those stones in," Riley said.

"That's a lot of work," Juan Carlo commented.

Frank handed Riley his oar. "Keep the boat close while Anthony and I check it out."

"Be careful," Riley warned Frank.

Frank stepped off the boat, his foot sinking into the muck. He swung his other leg over the side of the boat, stretching forward. His foot hit something solid. Frank grabbed a tree branch and pulled himself upright.

"It's not too bad here," he said to Anthony. "There's a bit of land here and there. It's muddy, though.

Try and stay on the tree roots."

Anthony followed. "Ew," he said as his feet slipped in the oozing mess.

Noah snickered.

"Don't laugh too hard," Anthony grinned at him. "I might pull you in, little bro." Anthony slipped again, dropping his hand into the muck to keep from falling down. He lifted a muddy hand and wiped it on a tree trunk.

Noah hooted with laughter. Then a howl broke through the trees. Noah's laugh died in his throat.

CHAPTER FIFTEEN

SMUGGLER'S DEN

Frank froze. "What *is* that?"

Anthony's shoulders tensed. He crept over to Frank. "Is something here?" he whispered.

Frank looked around. "Let's check the fireplace and get out of here."

The two men advanced to the fireplace, carefully stepping to find solid purchases for their feet. Frank touched the side of the fireplace. Then he pushed at some stones. "It seems solid enough." His voice carried back to the boat.

"Yeah, but the ground's not too firm." Anthony walked gingerly around the fireplace, trying to step on tree roots instead of muck.

Frank stooped down and crawled into the fireplace.

"I can't find anything," Anthony said. "There's nothing out here that would be a hiding place."

"I don't see anything, either," Frank's voice echoed from the chimney. "But I'm too big to check the stones up higher."

Frank stepped back out of the fireplace and joined

Anthony, who had made his way around the entire structure.

"How do we check high up on the inside?" Frank asked. "That's the logical place to hide something."

Anthony stepped back, stumbling into the mire. "Man," he grumbled, lifting up a wet shoe.

"I can go up there," Noah hollered at them.

Frank put his hands on his hips. He eyed Riley, who finally nodded. "Okay," he said.

"Be careful," Riley said as she helped Noah from the boat.

Noah hopped on a tree root and balanced himself. Then he skipped from dry spot to dry spot, tentatively making his way over to Anthony and his dad.

A wail pierced the silence. Noah stopped mid-step.

"Who's there?" Frank shouted. He glanced around uneasily. "That sounded close." He poked his head into the fireplace. "I wonder if it's coming down the flue." He ducked back into the fireplace and stood up. He placed a foot on a stone and climbed up a couple of feet.

"Come on, it's okay," Anthony beckoned for Noah to move forward.

Noah gulped and then bounded quickly over to him.

"Whoa." Noah stumbled. He threw out a hand and grabbed Anthony. "How did anyone ever live here?"

"It was probably much drier a long time ago," Anthony said.

"I'll get stuck if I go any farther. My shoulders are too wide," Frank's voice came from inside the chimney. "Anthony, where's the flashlight?"

Anthony reddened. "I didn't bring it."

"Well, go get it," Frank said, exasperated.

Anthony rushed as quickly as he could back to the boat.

"Noah, Anthony and I will lift you up into the chimney," Frank said. "Check for loose stones, just be careful not to drop any on us."

"Okay."

Noah backed up, trying to see the top of the chimney. He lost his balance and tumbled back into the underbrush. He got to his knees and started to stand up. But something tugged at his leg. It jerked him and Noah fell facedown into muddy water. Noah pushed himself to his knees again, gasping. He wiped at his face and looked down.

A Burmese python the size of a telephone pole had wrapped itself around his leg! Noah saw the python's skin, which was covered in brown blotches bordered in black. It had to be over ten feet long!

"Dad!" Noah screamed as the python curled around his waist.

Frank ducked down, staring out of the fireplace opening. His jaw dropped when he saw Noah with the snake wrapped around him.

"Noah!" Frank stood up quickly and whacked his

head on the stone fireplace. He dropped backward, momentarily dazed.

"Help!" Noah pulled at the thick snake's body as it squeezed him. He knew that a python killed its prey by constricting its strong muscles until its victim couldn't breathe. Noah pushed helplessly at the snake's body. It was too big and too strong. He could feel the snake crushing his ribs.

"Hey!" Anthony leaped at them.

He grabbed the snake's head and pulled it backward. But the python continued to wrap around Noah.

"Can't...get...out," Noah wheezed.

Anthony fell to the side as the snake whipped its head around. Its muscles relaxed momentarily and Noah slid toward the ground. But then the snake constricted again.

"We have to unwind it!" Frank yelled.

He raced over and pulled at the python's tail. The snake thrashed, but the two men overpowered the snake and it quickly unwound from Noah's waist. Noah twisted himself a bit, finally tumbling out of the python's grip.

"Oof." Noah landed hard in the brush and backed away from them.

"I've got its head," Anthony yelled. The snake calmed a bit. "Get his lower body."

Frank grabbed the snake's middle. The two men

hauled the snake to the other side of the island, grunting and lurching in the uneven soil. With a heave, they threw the python into the brush. It slithered away.

Frank rushed back to Noah. "Are you okay?" he said as he pulled Noah into his arms. Riley ran up, her jeans muddy from tumbling in the swamp.

"I'm okay," Noah said, fighting not to tremble.

"That was too close," Anthony said, breathing heavily. "You must've stepped on it."

Noah nodded. "I knew they lived in the 'Glades, but I've never seen one."

"Frank, this is too much," Riley said. "We need to go back."

"No!" Noah protested. "We've come this far, we can't stop."

Frank looked over at Juan Carlo. He was sitting in the boat, relief etched on his face. "Noah should come back to the boat," Juan Carlo said.

"We can do this," Noah ignored Juan Carlo. "Dad, you hoist me up into the chimney and I'll check the higher stones. Mom, you and Anthony watch for that snake…or any others."

"He's right," Anthony said. "We've come too far to give up now."

"Okay." Frank strode back to the fireplace, followed by the others. "Where's the flashlight?"

Anthony hurried to where he had dropped it when he helped rescue Noah from the snake.

"Here." He handed it to Noah. It was small and lightweight, perfect for Noah's smaller hands. "Hurry."

Frank and Noah crawled into the fireplace. Noah turned on the light as Frank wrapped his arms around Noah's knees. Frank raised Noah up into the narrow part of the chimney.

"Can you move?" Frank asked.

"Yes." Noah had about six inches all around his body. He shone the light around, searching for any loose stones. He saw one and reached up for it with one hand. He worked at the stone until it came out. Putting the flashlight in his mouth, he felt around with his other hand. Nothing. He put the stone back and repeated the process a few times. His shoulder began to ache.

"Anything?" Frank asked. He shifted and Noah bumped his elbow on a stone.

"No," Noah mumbled around the flashlight.

"Ooooooohhh," a low wail sounded right in Noah's ear. He stiffened.

"Dad," Noah whispered. "It's right here."

"It's okay," Frank said. "There are no ghosts around."

The moan sounded again.

"It's coming from right above me." Noah peeked above him. "It's too dark to see."

"Shine your flashlight where you hear the sound," Frank instructed him.

Noah pulled his arm up, took the flashlight from

his mouth, and shone it above him. He spied a crack in the stones. He reached up to feel in it, then stopped. *What if something's in there?* he thought. Then he took a deep breath and poked his hand in the crack. Nothing bit at his hands. But Noah could feel air coming through the crack. Then the wail startled him. This time, Noah covered the crack with his hand. The wailing stopped. He moved his hand and the sound returned. He put his hand over it again, and the sound stopped.

"What is it?" Frank asked.

"The breeze is blowing through a crack in the chimney," Noah said. "That's what's causing the noise!"

Frank laughed. "There's your ghost."

Relieved to know what was making the sound, Noah continued his search. He couldn't see any other loose stones so he started pushing at them one by one with his hand. Dust and ash filtered down around him. He sneezed and coughed.

"Anything?" Frank repeated.

"Push me higher."

Frank shoved him upward. Noah banged his sore shoulder. "Ow!"

"What?" There was fear in Frank's voice.

"Nothing. My shoulder."

Noah kept on, but he was growing discouraged. Had he brought everyone out here on a wild goose chase? He was the one who thought the emerald could be hidden in the chimney.

"What a dumb thought," he murmured, slamming a fist against a stone.

It moved slightly. Noah pushed with his fingers. The stone was loose, much looser than the others he'd checked. It didn't fit snugly with the other stones. He pulled at it and it suddenly popped out completely.

"Watch out!" he yelled, trying to catch it. He caught it momentarily by pressing it between his body and the chimney wall, but then it slid down.

"Ouch! It hit my foot," Frank yelped.

"Sorry." Noah reached into the empty space where the stone was. He felt something metal. He barely breathed as his fingers closed around what felt like a small box.

"I've got something," he said excitedly.

Frank lowered him down. Noah's feet touched the ground and he scrambled out of the fireplace. Frank ducked out after him and everyone stood around Noah.

"Open it," Riley said.

Noah unclasped a tiny lock and opened the box. Inside was something covered in tattered leather. Noah dumped the contents out of the box. A large green gem tumbled into his hand. Noah held the gem up to a ray of sunlight. It glinted brilliantly.

"It's beautiful," Riley said softly.

"Wow," Anthony said.

"Is that it?" Juan Carlo shouted from the boat. "Did you find it?"

"Yes!" Frank picked up the emerald and held it up for Juan Carlo to see. "We've got it!" he yelled jubilantly.

"And now I will take it from you."

Max Scheff emerged from behind the stone fireplace.

CHAPTER SIXTEEN

GREAT CATCH!

Max held an assault rifle. Behind him stood Dave 'The Wrench' Dixon. He had a bump the size of a crabapple on his forehead.

"How did you find us?" Frank asked Max.

"We put a bug in the spyglass," Max replied. "Just in case you did escape. We've tracked your location since you left the Copper Key. I know you, Frank." He nodded at Riley. "And you, too. We've worked against each other for so many years, searching after the same treasures. I could tell you what you'd do before you even think of it. I knew you'd keep the spyglass with you at all times."

"Ever since you stole the French Diamond from us, we've had to be extra careful," Frank said.

"But you've never resorted to threatening us," Riley said. "Or kidnapping."

"That wasn't me," Max snapped. "That was Isaiah Wright."

"It doesn't matter," Frank said. "We have the emerald."

"Not anymore." Max took a step forward. "Give it to me."

Noah clutched it in his hand. "No. We found it. It belongs to Juan Carlo."

Max turned and looked at Frank. "Do you want to tell him to give me the emerald, or should I? I guarantee that I'll be much more persuasive."

"Let him have it, Noah," Frank said.

Off to the left, something rustled in the brush. Dave whirled around, gun pointed at the disturbance. Max kept his gun trained on the Winters and Anthony.

"Relax, Dave," Max said. "Frank here just threw something over there to distract us."

Frank raised an eyebrow. "No, I didn't."

Uncertainty crossed Max's face.

"You think you know all my moves, but that's one I didn't make," Frank said.

"We had a fight with a python a few minute ago," Anthony said. "Maybe it's come back."

Max laughed. "You're not going to scare us." He pointed the rifle at Noah. "Give me the emerald."

Noah stepped forward and handed the jewel to Max. Max held it up, twisting it in his fingers.

"Stunning," he said. "I can't believe it's real."

A crunching sound came again, but this time a long, steel-gray body slithered out of the underbrush. Its long tail whipped to the side, crushing sawgrass. It snapped its jaw, teeth flashing dangerously.

"Max," Dave said fearfully.

An alligator stared at them all. Then he inched toward Max and Dave.

"Shoot it," Max ordered Dave.

Dave lifted his rifle, but before he could fire, the alligator stormed at him. It seemed to Noah as if everything was happening in slow motion. He saw Dave jerk backward, bumping into Max. Max stumbled, his hands flailing. The rifle butt hit the ground near the alligator. It stuck in the mud, with the stock pointing skyward. The gator paused and stared at the rifle. The emerald flew out of Max's hand, high into the air, where it circled around, catching the beams of sunlight. Green sparkles danced around them. Then the emerald dropped toward the ground.

"No!" Riley cried out.

Noah reached out and caught the emerald.

"Great catch!" Anthony pumped his fist.

Everything sped up. The gator raced at Max and Dave. Dave snatched a tree branch and hauled himself up into the cypress. Max did the same, only he couldn't quite pull himself up. He clung to a branch, his legs dangling precariously close to the gator's snapping its jaws.

"Run!" Frank yelled. But Riley, Noah, and Anthony were already racing through the muck to the airboat. They all leaped aboard and Frank jumped in the elevated seat. Juan Carlo and Anthony grabbed the oars and they pushed away from the island.

Anthony looked back. "The gator's leaving them," he said, pushing with all his strength.

The boat crept agonizingly slowly out into the marsh. Noah stared back. Max and Dave dropped out of the tree and disappeared.

"Just a little farther," Juan Carlo said, helping Anthony push.

The boat slid into deeper water.

"Now, Frank," Riley hollered.

Frank pivoted the rudders. Just as he was about to fire up the engine, Noah heard the roar of another airboat engine.

"Max is coming," he shouted.

Frank nodded and the airboat powered to life. He worked the rudders as the boat picked up speed. They cut through the mucky water and into the sunshine. A sawgrass prairie surrounded them.

"There they are!" Noah pointed.

Max and Dave were in a similar airboat, barreling down on Noah and the others.

"Hang on!" Frank turned the boat. It tipped precariously, but continued on. Behind them, Max kept pace.

"Head toward that island," Anthony screamed over din of the fan.

Frank saw the island and some mangrove trees. He jerked the rudder and the boat careened to the right of the mangrove. The screeching sound of metal scraping the tree roots shuddered through the boat.

Noah glanced over his shoulder. Max tried to turn his airboat. It tipped toward the right. Then the airboat's portside clunked against the mangrove roots and jerked to a halt. The impact threw Max and Dave out of the boat. They tumbled head-over-heels into the marsh. Max stood up, dripping wet. He shook his fist at Noah and the others.

"He'll never catch us now!" Frank yelled.

The airboat flew through the sawgrass, heading back to Everglades City.

"Ha." Juan Carlo smiled triumphantly. "The emerald is back with my family."

CHAPTER SEVENTEEN

VIAL OF POISON

Later that night, Noah was dozing on the couch when Chief Burton came over for a visit.

"Don't get up," he said to Noah.

Riley led Chief Burton into the kitchen, where she and Frank were reliving the day's events. Anthony was asleep in his room, and Juan Carlo had already flown his private jet back to New York. But Juan Carlo promised that he would return in a couple of days to take the Winters and Anthony out for a celebratory dinner.

Noah yawned. Now that all the excitement was over, he was exhausted. But just hearing his parents talking made him happy. They were back safe at home again. And he had helped with that.

He rolled on his side and looked into the kitchen. Chief Burton was leaning against the counter with his arms crossed. Frank and Riley sat at the table.

"I got a warrant and this morning we searched Isaiah Wright's house and the island," Chief Burton said.

"And?" Riley asked.

Chief Burton shrugged. "We didn't find anything that would indicate you'd been held there."

"What about the motorcycle that Noah ran into the water?" Frank said.

"We searched along the coast, but it wasn't there," Chief Burton said. "We took Wright in for questioning, too. I talked to him for hours, but I couldn't get anything out of him. He denies any wrongdoing, and he says he's never heard of Max Scheff or Dave 'The Wrench' Dixon. Not only that, Wright said that you all had trespassed on his island and that he caught you. When he confronted you both, you stole the Slingshot and left the island. He and Chang were following so they could get their boat back."

"You know that's a lie," Frank said.

"Of course," Chief Burton said. "But it's because you're the ones telling me the story. If someone walked into the station and told me Wright had kidnapped them, I'd have my doubts. Isaiah Wright is eccentric, but he's never broken the law, and he's never been suspected of breaking the law."

"He's too rich to get caught," Riley snorted.

"That may be so," Chief Burton continued. "But until I can prove anything, I can't do any more. A man like Wright is too smart to have any evidence lying around. Although I don't know how much that will help. And Wright made an interesting comment right before Detective Shaw and I left."

Riley rubbed her eyes in frustration. "What's that?"

"Wright said that he could press charges against you for stealing his boat –"

"But that's preposterous!" Riley interrupted.

Chief Burton held up a hand to stop her. "No, Wright could do that. But he looked me square in the face and said that he wasn't going to do that because he didn't want any problems. He was clearly sending me a message. The police leave him alone, and he'll leave us alone."

"So Wright gets away," Riley said angrily.

"We'll keep an eye on him," Chief Burton said. "He'll have to be extra careful about what he does now. If he so much as jaywalks, I'll arrest him."

Riley frowned.

Chief Burton looked from Frank to Riley. "And there's another thing."

"What?" Frank asked.

"Say we did find something and we charged Wright. You would have to testify, and so would Noah. And then it would be Wright's word against Noah's. It could get ugly in court. And after all that Noah's been through, do you want to see him endure more from Wright?"

Frank crossed his arms. "You're probably right. I just hate to see Wright get away with this."

"I do, too," Chief Burton said. "But there's one

thing I believe after twenty years of law enforcement."

"What's that?" Riley asked.

"Kharma," Chief Burton smiled. "Someday, Isaiah Wright will get his reward."

Frank chuckled. "I hope you're right."

"You got the emerald. You won this round." Chief Burton headed out of the kitchen. "Come in tomorrow so I can get your statements."

Noah flipped over and pretended to sleep.

"Nice try." Chief Burton tapped Noah's head. Noah looked up sheepishly. "You stay out of trouble, you hear?"

"Yes, sir," Noah said.

"Will do." Frank shook Chief Burton's hand. "Thanks for everything."

Chief Burton whistled as he went out the front door.

***

Monday evening the following week, the Winters, Anthony and Juan Carlo arrived at the Key West Harbour Yacht Club, one of the best places to eat in Key West.

"I love their Key Lime pie," Noah whispered to Juan Carlo as the maître'd seated them.

"I must try that," Juan Carlo said.

Noah ordered sautéed yellowtail, his favorite fish.

"I took the emerald to be evaluated," Juan Carlo said. "It is estimated to be worth five million dollars."

"Are you going to sell it?" Noah asked.

"No," Juan Carlo said. "It will remain with my family. I am just glad to have it back and to know that Roberto De La Rosa was indeed a pirate." He smiled. "It makes my heritage that much more interesting, no?"

Noah nodded. "That's pretty cool, if you ask me."

Anthony laughed. The waiter delivered their entrees. Noah put his nose close to his dish and smelled the yellowtail. Living on a tiny island, he loved all the varieties of fish that he could eat.

"Before we start, I would like to offer a toast," Juan Carlo said, raising his glass.

Noah lifted up his water glass along with Frank, Riley, and Anthony.

"To the finest team of treasure hunters around," Juan Carlo said. "You have fulfilled an old man's dream."

"Thank you," Frank and Riley said together. Anthony smiled.

Juan Carlo tipped his head at Noah. "And to the bravest boy I have ever met."

Noah blushed. "Thank you," he murmured.

Everyone took a drink.

"What a week," Juan Carlo said, chuckling. He set his glass down.

"Let's eat!" Anthony said.

"All right." Noah dived into his yellowtail. It tasted as good as it ever had.

***

The next night, Noah was sitting on the couch with Anthony, watching TV.

"Hey, we have a surprise for you," Frank said as he came in from the kitchen. He handed Noah an envelope.

"What's this?" Noah asked.

"Open it," Riley said.

Noah opened the envelope. Inside was a brochure for a ski resort in Vail, Colorado. Noah took the brochure out and held it up. "Skiing?"

Riley smiled. "I think it's time for the boy with a cold weather name to actually see some winter, don't you think?"

Noah stared at her, speechless.

"But I don't know how to ski," he finally said.

Anthony laughed. "You water ski. Trust me, you'll pick up snow skiing. Or you can try snowboarding."

"Sound like fun?" Frank asked.

"Yeah!" Noah said.

"We figured you deserved a reward for all the help in finding the De La Rosa emerald," Riley said. "You have to keep up your grades, though, or no deal."

"I will," Noah promised.

"Hey, look at that." Anthony pointed at the television. On the screen was a picture of Isaiah Wright.

"Turn it up," Frank said.

Noah pushed a button on the remote.

"…was found dead in his home. Wright, an eccentric billionaire, owned Copper Key, nine miles past Key West. Authorities do not suspect foul play in Wright's death, although an autopsy will be performed. In other news…"

Anthony looked from Frank to Riley. "Do you think Max Scheff was involved in Wright's death?"

"I'll bet he used that poison," Noah said. Everyone stared at him. "I forgot to tell you that part," Noah continued, then explained about Wright's vial of poison.

Frank rubbed his chin when Noah finished. "If that's what happened, I'd say that Wright was rewarded for his actions."

"But what about Max Scheff?" Noah asked. "What will happen to him?"

"I'm sure we'll be seeing him again," Riley said. "Whatever treasure we go after, it seems Max is there, too."

Noah thought about Max. The man was certainly the formidable foe his parents said he was. And as Noah watched the rest of the news with his family, he knew that he would someday cross paths with Max Scheff again.

Noah Winter will soon be back in another exciting adventure! To find out when the next adventure is available, and for information on Renée's other books, contests, and freebies, sign up for email alerts at www.reneepawlish.com.

Biography

Renée Pawlish is the award-winning author of the bestselling *Nephilim Genesis of Evil*, the first in the Nephilim trilogy, the Reed Ferguson mystery series (*This Doesn't Happen In The Movies* and *Reel Estate Rip-off*), The Noah Winters Adventure series for young adults (*The Emerald Quest*), *Take Five*, a short story collection, and *The Sallie House: Exposing the Beast Within*, a nonfiction account of a haunted house investigation. She lives in Colorado.

Printed in Poland
by Amazon Fulfillment
Poland Sp. z o.o., Wrocław